A Robyn Hunter Mystery

Out of the Cold

NORAH McCLINTOCK

Scholastic Canada Ltd.
Toronto New York London Auckland Sydney
Mexico City New Delhi Hong Kong Buenos Aires

Scholastic Canada Ltd.
604 King Street West, Toronto, Ontario M5V 1E1, Canada

Scholastic Inc.
557 Broadway, New York, NY 10012, USA

Scholastic Australia Pty Limited
PO Box 579, Gosford, NSW 2250, Australia

Scholastic New Zealand Limited
Private Bag 94407, Greenmount, Auckland, New Zealand

Scholastic Children's Books
Euston House, 24 Eversholt Street, London NW1 1DB, UK

Library and Archives Canada Cataloguing in Publication
McClintock, Norah
Out of the cold / Norah McClintock.

(A Robyn Hunter mystery)
ISBN 978-0-545-99728-7

I. Title. II. Series: McClintock, Norah. Robyn Hunter mystery.
PS8575.C62O98 2007   jC813'.54   C2007-901039-3

ISBN-10: 0-545-99728-3

Cover photo by Catherine London.

6 5 4 3   Printed in Canada   08 09 10 11

To Mr. Jones

Chapter 1

My father's loft was as silent as a mortuary and as dark as the inside of a coffin — except for the glow from his study. I walked toward it.

The glow was coming from the screen of the computer that sat to the right of my father's desk. Staring out at me from the screen was a not-quite-right likeness of Ted Gold, the man my mother had been seeing for almost a year. My parents are divorced. Despite my mother's best efforts to keep her personal life, well, personal — according to her, the divorce had terminated my father's right to know — my father is well aware of Ted. He'd even met him a couple of times — *not* my mother's idea. I stared at the Ted-like picture on the screen and wondered what my father was up to. Knowing him, it was probably nothing my mother would approve of.

Somewhere in the enormous loft that my father calls home, something hit the floor with a bang.

I jumped.

My heart pounded as I called, "Dad?"

I poked my head out of his study just in time to see someone — not my father, but a woman I had never seen before — straighten up after picking up a heavy, hardcover book from the floor. She was wearing a bathrobe and had a towel wound around her head. She didn't look anywhere near as surprised to see me as I was to see her.

"You must be Robyn," she said, smiling. "Mac was hoping to be here when you arrived, but he called to say that he was running late." That was typical of my father. He has made a career out of being late for every conceivable type of occasion, from school concerts to wedding anniversary celebrations, which helps explain why he and my mother are no longer married. "He asked me to tell you he should be home by nine." She glanced at the clock on the mantelpiece. "Uh-oh. If I don't get going, *I'm* going to be late." She disappeared into what was supposed to be *my* room, but which I knew my father also used as a guest room. "Nice to meet you," she said as she closed the door.

Meet me? I still had no idea who she was. She hadn't even told me her name.

Okay, so a woman I had never seen before (an awfully *young* woman, if you ask me, considering that my father was firmly embedded in his forties) had apparently taken a shower, or maybe a bath, in my father's bathroom and was now getting dressed in my (part-time) bedroom. What was a girl — me — supposed to do in an awkward (for me, if not for her) situation like this?

I decided to bail.

I left my suitcase near the front door where I had dropped it and went downstairs to see if Nick was around.

I hadn't seen Nick in seven days — and before that, I hadn't seen him alone, just the two of us, in weeks. My mother claimed that she had nothing against Nick personally, but that didn't mean she considered him ideal boyfriend material for me. For one thing, Nick has had a few problems, some of them with the law. He also didn't have what my mother would consider the best family situation. Far from it. Both of his parents are dead. His stepfather and stepbrother were both in prison. Nick was supposed to be living with his aunt, but that hadn't worked out because Nick didn't get along with his aunt's new boyfriend. So for the last couple of months he'd been renting an apartment from my father, who owns a building that used to be a carpet factory. My father lives on the top floor. The first floor is occupied by a trendy gourmet restaurant called La Folie. The second floor consists of six apartments. Nick lived in one of them. My mother had never been comfortable with that.

She was much, much less comfortable after what had happened last month, before I went on a week-long school trip.

"You were almost killed," she'd said. "And it was all Nick's fault."

In fact, it wasn't *all* Nick's fault, but there was no point in arguing with my mother. And I hadn't been killed. Everything had worked out just fine. But that

3

hadn't stopped my mother from having a total melt-down. She had forbidden me to see Nick ever again. She had ordered my father to evict him and was furious when he refused. "Fine," she'd said. "Robyn is not setting foot in that building as long as that boy is there." I argued with her until I almost lost my voice. In the end, it was Ted who had negotiated a compromise — basically, a month of extremely lim-ited access to Nick that broke down like this: I wasn't allowed to see Nick or even talk to him for a whole week. For two weeks after that, I could only see him in my mother's or Ted's presence. Nick had been so uncomfortable after the first time that mostly we had just talked on the phone. Who could blame him? My mother had allowed him to come over to her house to watch a movie with me and then had sat in one corner of the room the whole time, supposedly reading, but really keeping a sharp eye on us. I had hoped my father would cut us some slack. He hadn't. Other than refusing to evict Nick, he had gone along with my mother. He didn't want to make waves. "Your mother has every right to be upset," he'd said.

For the final week, I was out of town. My mother had looked relieved when she saw me off on the bus.

But now, at long last, my punishment was over. I could see Nick whenever I wanted — without a chap-erone. I couldn't wait. I had called him a couple of times while I was out of town, but he hadn't answered his phone. He'd probably been working. Nick put in a lot of hours at a part-time job. He also went to school. That didn't leave him with a lot of spare time.

My heart was pounding as I knocked on his door.
There was no answer.

I knocked again.

Still no answer. He wasn't home.

I heard footsteps in the stairwell. Nick? But no, the footsteps were going in the wrong direction. Instead of coming up from street level, they were coming down from the third floor. It must be the mystery woman from my father's place. I waited in the second-floor hallway until I heard the door on the ground floor swoosh open and clang shut again. Then I went down to La Folie. Nick had landed a job there (thanks to my father) right after he had supposedly almost got me killed and right after he had broken his ankle. He was probably in La Folie's kitchen right now, perched on a stool, scraping plates and loading them into the industrial-sized dishwasher.

I was wrong.

"Isn't Nick working today?" I asked Lauren, the hostess.

She gave me a funny look. "No," she said. "He isn't." I was pretty sure she was going to say something else, but just then a party of six arrived and wanted to be seated. "Excuse me, Robyn," she said as she bustled away.

If Nick wasn't at home and he wasn't at work, maybe he was visiting his aunt. Or maybe he was just out. I went back up to my father's place and lugged my suitcase to my room. I'll say one thing for the mystery woman — she was neat. Everything was exactly as I had left it. You would never have known that she'd been there at all. I was on my way to the kitchen to make a cup of tea when I heard the door. It was my father. His face lit up when he saw me.

"Robbie! How was the trip?" he said. "Did you have a good time?"

I had spent the past week on what my school had billed as a cultural field trip, but there had been no fields involved. There hadn't even been any in the vicinity. This trip had been decidedly urban — three days of lectures and hands-on learning behind the scenes at a museum, two days of educational sight-seeing, and an evening at the theatre. My best friend Morgan had gone, too, and we had been billeted together, which meant, "I had a pretty good time, Dad."

My father was still smiling while he looked around. "Where's — "

"She said she had to run. Who is she, Dad?"

"Tara?"

So that was her name.

"Are you hungry?" my father said as he hung up his coat. "Because I'm starving."

"I'm fine." I followed him into the kitchen and took a seat at the counter while he rummaged around in the fridge. "So who exactly is she?"

Out came a chunk of cheese — extra-old cheddar, I think — and the end of a ham, followed by a jar of Dijon mustard, a tomato, half a loaf of dark bread — pumpernickel? — and a container of coleslaw. Finally he closed the fridge door.

"Sorry, did you say something, Robbie?"

"Tara — who is she?"

"She's a very old friend," he said, smiling. There was a twinkle in his eye that made me think he wasn't telling me everything.

"She doesn't look that old," I said. "In fact, she seems kind of young."

"Does she?" He pulled a knife from the drawer and sliced the tomato and then the ham. "I think she's just about right." He rinsed the knife and cut into the cheese. "Are you sure you're not hungry?"

"I'm sure. How long have you known her, Dad?"

"Long enough, I guess." He pulled out another knife and used it to spread one of the slices of bread with a thin layer of mustard. "Did you tell your mother you're back?"

"I called her as soon as the bus got in." Which reminded me. "Have you been snooping on Ted?"

He looked confused. Or maybe he was just *acting* confused. With my father, it's sometimes hard to tell.

"What do you mean?" he said.

"I saw a picture of him on your computer. Have you been checking up on him?" It wouldn't have surprised me. For some reason that I didn't quite understand, especially given how acrimonious the separation and divorce had been, my father still seems to be in love with my mother. It would be just like him to try to dig up some dirt on Ted that he could present to her. Well, good luck. Ted is a sweet, mild-mannered, all-round nice guy. If he had any secrets, they were far more likely to be along the lines

7

of anonymous donations to good causes than they were to involve scandals or indiscretions.

"Checking up on him? Why would I do that, Robbie?" my father said. He had been layering ham, cheese, and tomato onto the mustardy bread, but he stopped and looked me straight in the eye to show that he was innocent of any wrongdoing. The thing is, though, my father is pretty good at deceit. He's the first to admit that it's often necessary in his line of work. He had been a police officer for nearly twenty years. Now he runs his own private security and investigations business. He says that sometimes, if you want to get the truth out of a liar, you have to lie yourself. My mother sees it differently. She says that lying comes as naturally to my father as breathing does to the rest of the world. "I promised your mother that I wouldn't snoop into her affairs," he said. "And I always keep my word."

Uh-huh. I studied him for a moment, trying to decide if he actually expected me to believe that. Then he said, "Robyn, about Nick — "

"I was going to ask you about him," I said. "I went to look for him, but he wasn't home and he's not at work. I thought for sure he'd be here. Have you seen him?"

"You went downstairs?"

"Yeah, but he wasn't there."

"Did you talk to Fred?"

He meant Fred Smith, owner of La Folie.

"No, but I talked to Lauren," I said.

"What did she say?"

"That Nick wasn't working today." Wait a minute. "Did you just call me Robyn?" The last time my father had called me by my proper name instead of using my nickname was when he'd told me about the divorce. "Is something wrong? Did something happen to Nick?"

My father dropped the top piece of bread onto his sandwich.

"I wish I knew," he said. He cut the sandwich in half, carried it and the container of coleslaw over to the counter, and sat down opposite me. "I haven't seen him since you left for that school trip."

"What do you mean, you haven't seen him? You mean he hasn't been home?"

My father laid a hand on my shoulder. Uh-oh.

"Dad, where's Nick?"

"I don't know."

"What do you mean, you don't know?"

"He's gone, Robbie. I don't know where. I don't know why. I don't even know exactly when he left. All I know is, he's gone."

* * *

"Gone?" Morgan said at school the next day. "What do you mean, he's gone?"

"I mean, he's not here. He's someplace else."

"Someplace else *where?*"

That was the million-dollar question. I told Morgan everything I knew, which wasn't much. Two days before we got back from our trip, my father had been downstairs having lunch at La Folie. After he ate, he went back to the kitchen to say hi to Nick, but Nick wasn't there. When my father asked Fred Smith how Nick was doing, Fred told him that Nick didn't work there anymore.

"Did he get fired?" Morgan said.

"He quit." Fred had told my father that Nick was nice about it. He thanked Fred for giving him a job and apologized for leaving on such short notice.

"He didn't say why he was quitting?" Morgan said.

I looked grimly at Morgan. "He said he was going out of town."

"Why? For how long?"

"Fred didn't ask, and Nick didn't say."

"What about your dad? Didn't Nick say anything to him?"

I shook my head. "My dad checked Nick's apartment after he talked to Fred. Most of Nick's things are gone." He'd left his furniture, almost all of which my father had given to him, and the few kitchen things he owned — dishes, a couple of pots, some cutlery, all bought at thrift stores — but he had taken his clothes and his more personal possessions.

"I don't get it," Morgan said. "Why didn't he call you and tell you where he was going?"

I had asked myself the same question a hundred times.

"Didn't he even leave you a note?" Morgan said.

"If he did, he wrote it in invisible ink on invisible paper."

"You don't think he's in trouble, do you?"

All I could do was shrug. Then I said what had been on my mind all night. "Morgan, what if he left because he didn't think he had any reason to stay?"

"What do you mean?"

"He's not getting along with his aunt. Joey's in prison." Joey was Nick's stepbrother. "Angie and the baby don't live here anymore." Angie was Joey's girl-friend. She had recently had a baby boy. "And he wasn't allowed to see me unless either my mother or Ted was right there with us. He didn't like that. And he knows how my mother feels about him. What if he got fed up?" Nick had had problems controlling his anger in the past. I was pretty sure he resented the way my mother had been treating him. Maybe he'd decided that putting up with her just to be with me wasn't worth it. Or maybe — I hated to think about it, but it was possible — maybe he'd met someone else.

"He knows you were away." Morgan said. "He knows when you were supposed to be back. If he cares about you, Robyn, he'll call."

If he cared so much, why hadn't he told me he was leaving? Why hadn't he called me already?

* * *

I got the key to Nick's apartment from my father and checked the place myself after school. Apart from a film of dust that had accumulated since he'd left, the place was spotless. I looked for a note but didn't find one. I even checked under the furniture in case it had fallen behind a dresser or under a table. Nothing. He was really gone.

I called Nick's Aunt Beverly and asked if she knew where he was.

"Why?" she said. "He isn't in trouble again, is he?

Don't tell me he got fired from another job."

He obviously hadn't told her that he was leaving, either. I said that I had been out of town and that I was trying to track him down. I didn't have the heart to say anything else.

I went to the group home where Nick had been living when I first met him. It was for kids who had been in trouble with the law and who had been sentenced to open custody — no locks, no bars, just strict discipline, lots of chores, and special programs in life skills and anger management. Nick had at least one friend there, a guy named Antoine, whom I'd met during the summer. Maybe he knew where Nick was.

"Sorry," the woman who answered the door told me. "Antoine isn't here anymore."

"Do you know where I can find him?"

"I'm afraid I'm not at liberty to give out that information."

Judging by her sombre expression, wherever Antoine was, *he* wasn't at liberty. Otherwise she would have told me.

For the next couple of days, I jumped every time my cell phone or the phone at my mother's house rang. When my mother finally said, "For heaven's sake, Robyn, relax," I burst into tears. My mother gave me a sympathetic look. She said she was sorry that Nick had taken off without a word. She said she understood how I must feel. She was trying to be nice, but I couldn't help thinking that she was relieved that Nick was out of my life. Then she said the very last thing that I wanted to hear. She said, "Maybe it's for the best."

* * *

"I still don't understand," I said. "Should I have done something different? Should I have snuck out to see him?" My mother would have grounded me for life if she'd found out I'd done that.

"It was only a few weeks, Robyn," Morgan said. "It wasn't exactly the end of the world. And you said you talked to him on the phone almost every day before the school trip."

"I thought if I did what my mother wanted — if we both did — she would see that he was okay. She would relax. I was more worried about what she thought than about what Nick thought."

I didn't mean to cry again, especially not in the school cafeteria where everyone could see me. But every time I thought about Nick, tears burbled up and I felt hurt all over again. Why had he taken off? Why hadn't he told me where he was going? Why hadn't he at least left a note?

"What if something has happened to him? What if he's met someone else? What if — ?"

Morgan pulled a wad of tissues out of her purse and thrust them at me.

"I like Nick," she said. "You know I do."

In fact, I didn't know that. I knew she thought he was good-looking, which he is — tall and lean, with jet-black hair and startling purple-blue eyes. I knew she thought he was exciting and kind of dangerous — mostly because of all the trouble he had been in and because of the hairline scar that runs diagonally across his face from the bridge of his nose to the bottom of his right ear. It makes him look like the kind of person who doesn't shy away from a fight. And it's true. He doesn't. I also knew that she respected the fact that I liked him, a *lot*. But, no, I didn't know that she actually liked him.

"But," she said — the word I had been waiting for — "you haven't known him for very long, which means that you may not know him as well as you think you do."

"What are you saying, Morgan?"

"There could be a dozen reasons he left — and why he didn't tell you. Until you hear from him, there's nothing you can do. You just have to wait."

"For how long?"

"I don't know." She squeezed my hand. "But I do know that whatever happens, it's not your fault. You didn't do anything wrong. If he wasn't prepared to wait a couple of weeks for you, that's his problem, not yours. I also know that if worst comes to worst, you can't keep crying over him. And don't give me that look, Robyn. You know what I mean. It's been almost a whole week since we got back and two weeks since he took off."

"Hey, guys," a cheery male voice said. I looked up. It was Billy Royal, my other best friend in the whole world and, recently, Morgan's boyfriend. He slipped an arm around Morgan and kissed her on the cheek before dropping into the empty chair beside her. "What's up?"

"Robyn is still beating herself up over Nick's disappearance," Morgan said, as if I were doing something wrong.

Billy gave me a sympathetic look. "Still haven't heard from him, huh?"

I shook my head.

"She needs to get her mind off him," Morgan said.

"I don't *want* to get my mind off him," I said. "I want to know where he is and why he left."

"What I mean is, you need to get your mind off thinking about him *all the time*," Morgan said. "It'll drive you crazy. You need to get busy with something."

"Why don't you come to the drop-in centre with Morgan and me?" Billy said. "They can always use extra help."

Billy volunteered at a drop-in centre for the homeless. He also volunteered at an animal rights organization and at the Humane Society, and was a founder of and the most active member in the Downtown Avian Rescue Club, which rescued injured migratory birds. Needless to say, he's a vegan.

"I don't know," I said. I admire Billy, but the way I was feeling, I would probably just depress the destitute.

"Seriously, Robyn, you should try it," Billy said. "The best way I know to feel good about yourself is to help someone else. Isn't that right, Morgan?"

Morgan nodded. "Although, to be honest," she said, "I feel just fine about myself."

I was sure that was true. Morgan was not given to

self-doubt, self-pity, self-loathing or, especially, self-criticism. The person who liked Morgan best was Morgan herself. Billy was her number two admirer.

"We're going down there tomorrow, right, Morgan?" Billy said. "And I know they're looking for more volunteers. The colder it gets, the more people use the drop-in centre." It was really cold now, and the nights were long and getting longer. It was pitch dark by five o'clock in the afternoon. "They need as many people as they can get to make soup and sandwiches, set out coffee, clean up after meals, sort and hand out donations of warm clothing and sleeping bags — stuff like that. It'll make you feel better. And you'll meet a lot of interesting people. Who knows? You might be surprised by what goes on down there. Come on, Robyn. What do you say?"

I wanted to say no. I didn't feel like doing anything. But Billy was so enthusiastic and he made it sound as if I'd be welcomed with open arms, so instead I said yes.

Billy beamed at me. "It's a great place to volunteer, Robyn. You won't regret it."

As it turned out, he was wrong. It wasn't long before I was sorry I had ever agreed.

Chapter 2

The way we had arranged it: I would meet Morgan and Billy at the drop-in centre, Billy would introduce me to the director, and the director would assign me something to do.

The change in plans: While I was waiting for the bus, Morgan called me on my cell phone and said she couldn't make it after all because she had woken up with a really bad sore throat. She said they didn't like people to volunteer at the drop-in centre if they were even remotely sick because a lot of the homeless people who used the centre weren't in the best of health. Some of them had immune systems that were seriously out of whack. But, she said, Billy was on his way, he was excited that I was going to join him, and he was dying to show me around.

The way it actually happened: I got off the bus where Billy had told me to. I could have waited for a second bus, but it wasn't due for another ten minutes. It wouldn't take that long to walk to the drop-in centre, and walking would help me to stay warm. At first I was walking past downtown stores, office buildings, and restaurants. Even there I kept running into people who were down and out. I'd only gone half a block before a grubby young man sitting in the doorway of a vacant store asked me for money. He was half-wrapped in a weathered sleeping bag that was torn in several places and he kept his eyes on the ground when I dropped a loonie and some quarters into a plastic cup on the sidewalk in front of him. One block farther on I passed a man with one leg who was leaning against a utility pole. He was holding out an empty margarine container, and muttering, "Sparechangesparechangesparechange," over and over in a whispery voice. I shrugged apologetically. I had already given all my coins to the young guy in the doorway.

On the next block, an old man sitting in front of an office building was cursing at a well-dressed man who was digging into his pocket for his wallet. He dropped a five-dollar bill into an upturned hat on the sidewalk, but even though that was more than most people gave, it didn't silence the old man. He kept right on cursing. I glanced at him and gasped involuntarily when he looked up at me. A jagged red scar slashed through his left eyebrow and ended halfway down his cheek. His left eye looked twisted. When I stared at him, wondering if he was blind in that eye, he started to curse at me, too. The well-dressed man gave me a sympathetic look before he turned and walked away. I picked up my pace and wondered what had made Billy and

Morgan think this would cheer me up.

The scenery changed rapidly after that, and I soon found myself in depressing surroundings. The drop-in centre was located in a rundown part of the city a couple of blocks away from a sprawling low-income housing project. Just as I was about to turn the corner, a woman in a puffy coat and tattered sneakers started screaming at me. At least, that's what I thought she was doing. It turned out that she was just plain screaming — and swearing — and that it had nothing to do with me. She shoved past me, pushing a shopping cart heaped with what looked like garbage, shouting and cursing and looking ferocious.

I arrived at my destination five minutes early. Even though the temperature was well below zero and the sky was a gloomy lead-grey, a loose group of men in grime- and grease-encrusted coats, most of them with dirty hair and scraggly beards, crowded the sidewalk in front of the church hall that housed the drop-in centre. At first I couldn't figure out why they were standing out in the icy cold when they could have been inside where it was warm. Then I noticed that almost all of them were smoking. Billy had told me that the drop-in centre enforced a strict no-smoking policy, so people who wanted a cigarette had to go outside. Most of the smokers ignored me. But a couple of them gave me a once-over as I made my way to the door. One of them said something I didn't quite catch to a second man, and the second man responded with a laugh that was as crusty as his coat.

I opened the door, stepped inside, and was immediately overwhelmed by the heat and by the stench of unwashed bodies, stale tobacco, and bad breath that mingled with the aroma of coffee and food cooking. I had never smelled anything quite like it. I wondered if Billy hadn't mentioned the smell on purpose or if he had gotten used to it. I was surprised that Morgan hadn't said something about it. There was no way she would have gotten used to it.

From what I could see from the main entrance, the drop-in centre took up the whole church hall and consisted of one enormous room that had been divided into several areas, as well as a kitchen — which I spotted when someone bustled through a door on the far side of the hall — and several smaller rooms. Two of the smaller rooms looked like offices. One was set up as a meeting room of some kind.

I looked around the large main room. In the area farthest from the entrance, some battered armchairs and two sagging couches sat clustered around a television set that was tuned to a talk show. Most of the chairs and sofas were occupied. A few people, mostly women, each with a bundle buggy parked nearby, were watching the TV or, at least, staring at the screen. A few others appeared to be asleep. The rest of the people were talking, some to each other, a few to themselves.

Another part of the room was set up with a long wooden table and folding chairs where people sat hunched over orange plastic trays that held bowls of cereal, mugs of coffee, and plates of toast. Along one wall, a woman — a volunteer? — was handing out plastic-wrapped sandwiches and containers of soup. Coffee was self-serve from a huge urn set up on another, smaller table.

The third and final area consisted of a half-dozen card tables ringed with folding chairs, some raggedy armchairs, and a small bookshelf that was crammed with paperback books. Decks of cards, a couple of cribbage boards, and some chess and checker sets sat on top of the bookshelf. A group of men sat around one of the tables playing cards.

I didn't see Billy anywhere.

Then a hand fell on my shoulder and I jumped. I turned and looked into the lined and weathered face of a man in faded jeans and a frayed denim shirt. His long grey hair was pulled back into a ponytail. He smelled of soap and aftershave lotion.

"You look lost," he said.

"I'm looking for Billy Royal," I said. "I'm supposed to meet him here."

The man smiled. "You must be Robyn. Billy called. I'm afraid he's had a change of plans. I'm Art Donovan. I run this place." He thrust out a hand and we shook. "Are you handy in the kitchen?"

I nodded.

"Great. I'll have someone show you around. Then, if you don't mind, I'll put you to work in the kitchen." He raised an arm and snapped his fingers. "Ben!" he called. "Ben, over here."

At first I thought that all of the men sitting at the card table must be named Ben, because they all turned to look at Mr. Donovan. Then one of the card players, younger and better dressed than the others, got up and loped toward us.

"Robyn, this is Ben Logan," Mr. Donovan said. "Ben, meet Robyn . . ."

"Hunter," I said, supplying my last name.

"Robyn is here for the day," Mr. Donovan said. "Who knows, maybe she'll like it so much that she'll decide to come back. Do me a favour. Show her around. Then take her in to Betty." He smiled at me. "Betty can always use an extra hand. Welcome aboard, Robyn." He left me with Ben.

Ben looked me over.

"Nice boots," he said.

I glanced down at my feet. "Thanks," I said. They were brand new and I loved them, but, boy, my mother had really grumbled about the price.

"Nice jacket, too," Ben said. It was also new, and amazingly warm. "Looks expensive." He made it sound like that was a bad thing. His eyes shifted to the gold earrings my father had given me for my birthday and then to my new sweater.

While he was inspecting me, I checked him out. Like Art Donovan, he was wearing faded blue jeans. He also had on a pullover sweater that had seen better days and a pair of beat-up sneakers. I started to feel self-conscious. Compared to him — in fact, compared to everyone in the place — I was seriously overdressed.

"Come on, I'll give you the grand tour," he said. The look on his face made me think that he would rather be scrubbing toilets than escorting me around. First he showed me where the various offices were — one for Mr. Donovan right off the main hall, one for a nurse who came by regularly, and, down a short hallway, one for a social worker who helped people get the things they needed. There was also a workspace with a couple of computers in it that people who visited the drop-in centre could use to access the Internet. Then he led me to the far end of the room, where a cooking show had come on the TV. Nobody was talking now.

Ben nudged me over beside the TV and said, in a loud voice, "Hey, everyone, this is Robyn."

A couple of people pulled their eyes away from the TV just long enough to give me a once-over. The rest of them remained focused on the cooking show.

Next he led me to the long table where a dozen or so people were spooning up milky oatmeal. One man was dunking pieces of toast into a mug of coffee and — yuck! — sucking on them. He had very few teeth that I could see.

"Hey, everyone," Ben said again, "this is Robyn." A few pairs of eyes looked from breakfast to me. One of them was the scruffy young man I'd given money to in front of the vacant store. His hands were wrapped around a mug of coffee. He stared at my boots and frowned when Ben introduced me. Ben shrugged at the lack of response. "You can see how excited everyone is to meet a brand new two-four," he said. There was an edge of sarcasm to his voice.

"A two-four?" I said.

"As in twenty-four — hours. Two-fours are one-day wonders. We get them around here all the time. Kids who have to put in a few hours of community service for school. People who drop by once a year, usually to serve Christmas dinner, so that their consciences won't bother them too much for having scored some Gucci or Prada or Louis Vuitton on Christmas morning. Come on, I'll show you the rest of the place, so you can tell your friends what a drop-in centre for the homeless looks like — that is, assuming your friends are interested in anything besides shopping."

I stared at him. "Where do you get off talking to me like that?" I said. "You don't know anything about me."

He looked me over again, pausing to stare pointedly at my earrings, my jacket, my boots.

"I see," I said. "You think that because of the way I dress — " I looked just as pointedly at his own shabby attire " — I don't care about these people. Is that it?"

As soon as I said "these people," a few people looked up at me from coffee mugs and cereal bowls. Great, I'd probably offended them.

"Is that why you're here?" he said. "Because you care so much?"

I wished I could say that that was exactly why I was there, but it wasn't. There was no way I was going to admit that to him, though. "I'm here because my friend Billy volunteers here and he told me they're always looking for more help," I said stiffly.

"Billy?" He sounded surprised. "Billy Royal?"

I nodded.

"*You're* a friend of Billy's?" He looked as astonished as if he'd just witnessed Billy sinking his teeth into a thick, juicy steak.

"Since kindergarten," I said.

"Hey, I'm sorry. I didn't know. I thought you were — "

"A two-four. Yeah. I got that. Mr. Donovan said they could use some help in the kitchen, so if you'll excuse me . . . " And even if you won't, I thought. I turned, went into the kitchen, and introduced myself to a woman who turned out to be Betty. She was standing in front of a counter, shelling what looked like several dozen hard-boiled eggs. A huge pot of soup simmered on the stove beside her.

"Can you follow a recipe?" she said.

I told her I could.

She gestured to a binder on the counter.

"We do three kinds of cookies — oatmeal raisin, chocolate chip, and molasses spice. I need twelve dozen of each."

"Twelve *dozen?*"

"Of each."

"But that makes . . . " My math failed me.

"Four hundred and thirty-two cookies. That should get us through the weekend."

Four hundred and thirty-two cookies would get them through the weekend?

"It would be a lot easier to just buy them," Betty said, reading my mind. "But these people don't eat right unless they're given good food. And I believe in good food, which includes cookies made with real eggs and without all those chemicals and preservatives they put in the store-bought ones. We get between eighty and one hundred people in here for dinner every day. Each person gets a piece of fruit and two cookies for dessert. That's one hundred and sixty to two hundred cookies per dinner. We also package some up to give to people who want to take a sandwich with them instead. And there are always people who sneak a few extras. The pans are there." She pointed. "Bowls, wooden spoons, measuring cups, and measuring spoons are all in there." She pointed to the far side of the room. "We can get twelve good-sized cookies on a pan, two pans in the oven at a time, fifteen minutes per batch."

That made . . . my math skills failed me again.

"That means four and a half hours just to bake the cookies. But first you have to mix the dough. Here's what you do . . . "

What you did, it turned out, was mix one batch of cookie dough — I started with oatmeal raisin — and scoop it out onto cookie sheets. Then, between popping batches of the first kind of cookie into the oven and taking them out again, I mixed up the second batch of cookie dough. Et cetera.

* * *

Two and a half hours and a mountain of cookies later, Betty said she was going outside for a smoke.

"Yes, I know smoking isn't good for me," she said. "Do you have any idea how many times I've tried to quit? Mind the store for me, will you, Robyn?" She pulled on a parka. "Clients aren't allowed in the kitchen. And absolutely no one is allowed into the basement." She nodded to the door that led down-stairs.

"Why don't you just keep it locked?" I said.

"Because all of my supplies are down there," she said. "And because Art is the only one who has a key. He says it's easier to control access that way. He unlocks the door when I come in and locks it again as soon as I'm finished for the day. It's strictly off-limits to clients. I'll be back in ten minutes."

I had just started to mix the molasses cookie dough when a raggedy old man shuffled into the room. At first I stared at his head. It was lopsided, as if some-where under his matted hair a piece of his skull was missing. Then I looked at his face — at the angry scar and the twisted left eye — and realized he was the same man I had seen out on the street, shouting at the man who had dropped a five-dollar bill into his hat.

Betty had told me that the kitchen was off-limits to people who used the drop-in centre — she called them clients. "If anyone comes in, politely ask them to leave," she had said. "If they won't leave, call Art."

The old man looked at the oatmeal raisin cookies that were sitting in big plastic containers on the coun-ters. I watched him and hoped that he would go away.

He didn't.

Instead, he started stuffing his pockets with cookies.

"Excuse me," I said, "but I don't think you're allowed to do that."

He stuffed more cookies into his pockets.

"Excuse me," I said again. I was thinking about all of the people who came to the drop-in centre for dinner every day. They probably looked forward to their cookies. "Excuse me, but you can't take those."

I started toward him — and stopped abruptly when he spun around to face me, his fists raised like a boxer. At first I thought it was kind of funny — this old man was trying to scare me so that he could filch some cookies, just like a little kid. Then I saw the wild look in his eyes, and I began to wonder if he might be dangerous.

He kept his fists up and stared belligerently at me. Then he took a step toward me.

I backed away. As soon as I did, he shuffled over to the counter on the other side of the kitchen where Betty had been cutting sandwiches in half and wrapping them in plastic. The knife she had been using was lying on a cutting board next to a bowl of shelled hard-boiled eggs. The old man's hand edged toward it. Was he going to pick it up? If he did, what did he plan to do with it? I glanced around frantically. Where was Betty? She must have finished her cigarette by now. She would know how to handle this.

The kitchen door opened. Betty, I thought thankfully.

But it wasn't her. It was Ben Logan.

"Look, I've been thinking — " He looked from me to the old man, who had grabbed not the knife, but a hard-boiled egg, and was stuffing it whole into his mouth. Ben shook his head. "Mr. Duffy, you're not supposed to be in here," he said patiently. He walked up to the old man and touched his arm. "Come on. Let's get you out of here before Betty comes back. You know what she's like when she finds people in her kitchen who aren't supposed to be here."

Ben tugged on Mr. Duffy's arm. I flinched as I pictured the old man whirling around and punching him in the nose or, worse, grabbing the knife and threatening him with it. But that's not what happened. Instead, Mr. Duffy allowed Ben to lead him to the kitchen door. Before they got there, the door swung open and Betty came in, unbuttoning her jacket. She shook her head when she saw the old man.

"What have you been up to, Mr. Duffy?" she said. When he didn't answer, she glanced at Ben, who merely shrugged. "Do I have to go through your pockets, Mr. Duffy?" Betty said.

Mr. Duffy stared at the floor. He didn't protest — he didn't even move — when Betty thrust a hand into one of his pockets.

"Mr. Duffy," she said, sounding as patient as Ben had, "you've been coming here long enough to know that there are only enough cookies to go around if everyone takes no more than his fair share." She pulled cookies out of one coat pocket and then another, and put them on the counter until they formed a small heap. She shook her head again.

"That's sixteen cookies, Mr. Duffy. Do you know

what Mr. Donovan would do if he found out you'd taken sixteen cookies?"

Mr. Duffy raised his head to look directly at her. He no longer seemed belligerent or dangerous. He smiled, almost as if he were trying to charm her. It worked. She sighed, gave him two cookies — one oatmeal raisin and one chocolate chip — and said, "Go along with Ben. And Ben? There's no need to mention this to anyone, okay?"

Ben nodded. Mr. Duffy followed him out of the kitchen.

"What *would* Mr. Donovan do if he found out?" I said.

"He'd probably bar him from the centre for a couple of days," Betty said. "Art tries to be understanding. We all do. Most of the people who use our services have a lot of problems, but most of them are reasonably well behaved and don't give us much trouble. There are a few, however, who sometimes act impulsively." From the way Betty had spoken to Mr. Duffy, I guessed he fit into the latter group. "But there are two things we can't put up with — theft of centre property, and violence. Everyone knows the rules and everyone knows why the rules are important." She looked at the cookies she had confiscated and, with a sigh, swept them into the garbage. "It's a waste, I know," she said, glancing at me. "Once he'd taken them, we might just as well have let him keep them for all the good they'll do anyone else. But rules are rules, and it's not fair to let one person get away with raiding the kitchen."

"Is there anything else I can do?" I said after I had packed the last cookie into one of the huge plastic bins Betty had set out.

"I'd say you've done more than enough for one day," Betty said. "You must be tired."

She was right. My feet hurt and my back ached from standing for hours. I washed my hands one final time, hung up my apron, and went to look for my jacket. I stopped on my way out to say goodbye to Art Donovan.

"Thanks for your help today, Robyn," he said. "I hope Betty didn't work you too hard."

"I'm glad I could help," I said. But I was already picturing myself soaking in a deep, hot bubble bath. "Billy is always saying that you need more volunteers."

"Billy's right," Mr. Donovan said. "In fact, I don't suppose you'd have any free time tomorrow," he said.

"Well I . . . " I didn't have any *definite* plans.

"We'll have more volunteers than we can handle come Christmas," he said. "But right now we're really short-handed. There are a couple of volunteers who usually help Betty in the kitchen, but one of them is out of town on a family emergency and the other one can't make it in tomorrow. What do you say?"

What could I say? I find it next to impossible to refuse when someone asks me for a favour, so I said yes.

"Terrific," Mr. Donovan said. "Wait a minute." He disappeared into a small office. When he returned, he handed me a sheet of paper. "Fill this out and bring it back with you tomorrow," he said. "It's a volunteer information form. We ask all volunteers to fill one out — basic personal information, who we should contact in case of emergency, that kind of thing. Okay?"

I nodded.

"Great," he said. "We'll see you tomorrow, then."

Twenty-four hours later, I was promising myself that I would learn how to say no.

Chapter 3

Billy was busy with his animal rights organization the next day, so he couldn't go to the drop-in centre. Morgan was still sick — at least, that's what she told me in a whispery poor-me-I've-got-a-sore-throat voice. So once again I headed downtown alone. And, wouldn't you know it, the first person I saw when I entered the church hall was Ben Logan. He was talking to the scruffy young guy I'd given money to. The guy pointed at me and said something to Ben, then put his hand up to cover his mouth. I could tell he was laughing. Ben laughed, too, and handed him something. I felt my cheeks burn. As I passed them, Ben said, "I didn't think you'd be back."

"I know," I said, without stopping. "Because you thought I was a two-four." I went directly into the kitchen, where Betty put me to work making and wrapping sandwiches. Ben showed up a few minutes later. I ignored him.

"Hey, come on," he said. "Aren't you going to talk to me?"

"I saw you laughing at me," I said.

"Laughing at you?" He gave me a baffled look.

"Just now," I said. "With that other guy."

"We weren't laughing at you."

"He pointed at me."

"He pointed at your boots."

Again with the boots. I remembered how he'd stared at them the day before, when Ben had showed me around. "He doesn't like them either, huh?"

"He didn't say," Ben said. "But they're how he recognized you."

"What? What are you talking about?"

"Andrew never makes eye contact when he's panhandling. But he sure knows his footwear. Yesterday when I was showing you around, he recognized your boots. He says you gave him money."

"And?" I said.

"And what?"

"What's so funny about my boots?"

"Nothing."

"You both laughed."

"True. But Andrew wasn't laughing at you. He was laughing at *me*."

"At you?" Did he actually expect me to believe that?

Ben shifted awkwardly.

"Andrew told me yesterday that I'm more prejudiced than some of the people who pass him on the street. He said they judge him by how he looks and that I did the same thing to you. He bet me that you weren't a two-four and that you'd be back."

"He did?"

Ben nodded.

"And he was right. Andrew enjoys being right. That's why he was laughing. Look, I'm sorry about the way I acted. I didn't know you were a friend of Billy's. And it's obvious you're not a two-four. At the very least, you're a four-eight." He grinned. When I just stared at him, he said, "It's a joke. Get it?"

"I get it," I said.

"So what do you say? Friends?"

After the way he had treated me?

"Okay, I guess I deserve that look," he said. "I was kind of obnoxious."

"Kind of?"

"I thought . . . well, you already know what I thought. If we can't be friends, can we at least agree not to be enemies? That way I might have a shot at convincing you what a great guy I really am."

Well, he was trying hard enough. And not only did he seem sincere, but he wasn't afraid to admit he was wrong. And it was obvious he thought highly of Billy. I relented just a little.

"I guess I could live with that," I said.

His whole face lit up, and I began to think he might not be so bad after all.

* * *

An hour later, I had made a couple dozen loaves of sandwiches — egg, peanut butter and jam, and tuna — and I was about to start on some ham and cheese when Betty was summoned to a meeting with Mr. Donovan.

A few minutes later after she'd left, while I was spreading mustard on the slices of bread I had laid out on the counter, someone darted through the kitchen door and disappeared into the basement.

I hesitated for a moment. Betty had told me that no one was allowed in the basement. I went to the top of the stairs.

"Hello?" I called. "Betty, is that you?"

No answer.

I heard a metallic *clunk* from somewhere down below. It sounded like someone was stacking cans of food. It had to be Betty. But why hadn't she answered? I started down the stairs. When I got to the bottom, I saw a man in a long, tattered overcoat, kneeling at the end of the shelves that covered one entire wall. It was Mr. Duffy. He was burrowing into a cardboard box.

"Excuse me," I said. After yesterday, I was a little afraid of him, so I stood well back. "Excuse me, but you're not supposed to be down here."

Mr. Duffy ignored me. He dipped into the box and started pulling out cans. I caught a glimpse of the labels. They were cans of peaches. He stuffed two into each of his coat pockets. I told myself that I should be understanding. After all, he was homeless and he was obviously hungry. But so was everyone else who used the drop-in centre. Stealing from the storeroom was the same as stealing from all of the people who relied on the centre for meals. It was against the rules. And hadn't Betty said that rules were rules? I remembered how she had handled the situation the day before. She had been patient, but firm.

"Mr. Duffy," I said, approaching him slowly. "You can't take those."

Mr. Duffy didn't react to me the way he had to Betty. Instead of being docile, he jumped to his feet and whirled around to face me. The expression on his scarred face was angry and hostile.

"Mr. Duffy, please," I said. It was all I had the chance to say. He looked at me, then at the stairs behind me. Then he rushed at me and pushed me hard, throwing me off balance. I reeled backward, stumbled over a box on the floor, and started to fall. My hands scrabbled for something to grab onto but didn't connect with anything. I landed with a crash. My head snapped back and hit the floor. I felt something sharp against the side of my face, close to my ear. For a moment I lay, dazed, on the concrete floor.

Mr. Duffy stood over me, his coat pockets bulging, a can of peaches clutched in each raised hand. I cringed, terrified that he was going to hurl the cans at me. But he didn't. Instead, he stepped over me and I heard him *thump-thump-thump* up the wooden stairs to the kitchen.

My head hurt. I felt disoriented, but I forced myself to sit up. The side of my face burned. I had to grip the wooden banister with both hands to steady myself as I staggered up the stairs. By the time I got to the top, Mr. Duffy was gone. Ben bustled through the kitchen door carrying a coffee urn. He stopped when he saw me and gave me a peculiar look.

"What happened to you?" he said.

"Did you see Mr. Duffy?" I said.

"Mr. Duffy? Why?"

"I caught him in the basement, stealing food. When I tried to stop him, he attacked me." My legs were trembling. My head was pounding. I felt dazed, and the side of my face felt like it was on fire. Mr. Duffy had really scared me. "Where's Mr. Donovan?" I said.

"I think he's in his office, but — "

I headed for the door.

"Whoa, wait," Ben said. He caught me by the arm. "You're bleeding."

"What?" My hand went to the right side of my face. When I pulled it away again, there was blood on my fingers. I bent down and twisted my head so that I could see my reflection in the side of the toaster oven on the counter. Blood was oozing out of what looked like a nasty gash on my face, close to my right ear. Blood had also soaked into the collar of my sweater. I felt faint at the sight of it and reached for the counter as my knees began to wobble.

Ben was beside me in an instant. He gently tucked my hair behind my right ear and pressed a clean towel against the wound. Still holding me with one hand, he snagged a chair with the other. "Sit," he said. He eased me down onto the chair. "Let me take a look." He pulled the towel away gingerly and then quickly pressed it back against my face. "I think you should get that looked at," he said. The sombre expression on his face scared me.

"How bad is it?"

"Where's your coat? I'll get a cab. We'll go to the hospital. It isn't far."

"But Mr. Donovan — "

"First things first," Ben said. "Wait here."

When he came back a few moments later, he was wearing his jacket and carrying mine. He helped me into it, told me to keep applying pressure to the wound, and whisked me out the side door. When we got to the street, he flagged a cab. Andrew, the scruffy young guy who had recognized me by my boots, was standing near the curb when Ben helped me into the taxi and told the driver he wanted to go to the nearest emergency room.

"Hey, Ben, is everything okay?" he said as Ben climbed into the taxi beside me. Ben didn't answer. He slammed the door shut and asked the driver to hurry.

We waited for nearly a half hour in the emergency department of the closest hospital. Ben kept getting up and going to the main desk to tell them that I was bleeding. Finally, a nurse led us to a small room where we waited some more until a doctor appeared and examined me. Diagnosis: a mild concussion (he handed me an information sheet on head injuries) and a facial laceration (why does *laceration* sound so much worse than *cut*?). "I'm going to put a couple of stitches in," the doctor said. The next thing I knew, he'd stuck a needle into my face. ("Local anaesthetic," he explained, right before he said, "This may pinch a little.")

"With any luck," he said when he had finished, "there won't be a scar."

Scar?

"And if you don't wear your hair back," he said cheerily, "no one will notice."

Right after the doctor finished with me, someone knocked on the door. It was Mr. Donovan. He glanced at Ben before asking if I was all right. I said I was, even though I felt woozy and my head still hurt, and all I could think about was the possibility that I'd end up with a scar on the side of my face. After I told him what the doctor had said and done, he came closer and looked at the bandage.

"I called your father," he said. I had listed him as my emergency contact on the volunteer information sheet. My father tends to be a lot calmer than my mother in tough situations, probably because he used to be a cop. "He's on his way here."

"How did you know where we were?" Ben said.

"Andrew saw you and Robyn leaving the centre in a taxi and heard you tell the driver that you wanted to go to the nearest emergency room. He said he thought Robyn had been hurt." Mr. Donovan gave Ben a sharp look. "You've been with us long enough to know the procedure, Ben. When someone is injured, I'm to be notified immediately."

He turned to me. "Do you want to tell me what happened, Robyn?"

"It was an accident," Ben said. "When I saw she was bleeding, I panicked." I looked at him. He had seemed perfectly calm and level-headed to me. "I decided I should get her to the hospital right away. I was going to call you."

"Wait outside, Ben. I'd like to talk to Robyn alone."

Ben's eyes caught mine and he stared hard at me, as if he were trying to tell me something. He nodded at Mr. Donovan and shook his head. What was that about? Then he went out into the hall. Mr. Donovan closed the door behind him and listened quietly while I told him what had happened. When I finished, he said, "Mr. Duffy can be a little unpredictable. I'm sorry. Do you want to press charges?"

"Press charges?" I said. I hadn't even considered that. "I don't think he meant to push me as hard as he did." At least, I hoped he hadn't. "I guess after what happened yesterday, he doesn't like me very much."

"Yesterday?" Mr. Donovan said.

Uh-oh. Betty had told Ben not to mention Mr. Duffy's cookie-stealing episode to anyone.

"What happened yesterday, Robyn?"

Mr. Duffy had stolen food. He'd done it twice now. Surely Mr. Donovan had a right to know. I told him what had happened.

"Ben says he's harmless," I added. "But, to be honest, he scares me a little."

"For the most part, Ben's right," Mr. Donovan said. "Don't worry, Robyn. I'll have a talk with Mr. Duffy."

My father arrived. Mr. Donovan spoke briefly to him. He asked my father the same thing he had asked me — whether he wanted to press charges. My father looked at me. I shook my head.

"If this man was violent toward you, Robbie, he

could be violent toward other people," my father said.

"He usually doesn't give us much trouble," Mr. Donovan said.

My father looked sceptically at him before turning back to me.

"Mr. Donovan is going to talk to him," I said.

"I'm going to make myself very clear," Mr. Donovan assured my father.

My father still looked doubtful, but he said the choice was mine. Just before Mr. Donovan left, he said, "I hope this won't stop you from volunteering with us again, Robyn." My father gave him a sharp look. After he left, my father inspected me.

"Your mother is going to be upset when she sees that," he said, bending down to take a closer look at the dressing on my face.

Talk about an understatement. She was going to freak out. She was already overprotective, especially after what had happened with Nick. This was only going to make things worse.

"Actually, Dad, I was hoping I could stay with you tonight."

"Sorry, Robbie, no can do."

"What do you mean, no can do?"

"You know I love it when you visit — "

"*Visit?* You told me when you and Mom split up that I would always be welcome at your place because it's my place, too. My second home."

"My place is your place, Robbie. But if I know your mother, she's already pacing up and down. You know what she's like. She's going to want to see for herself that you're all right."

"You *told* her?"

"I called the hospital on the way over to see how you were," my father said. "Then I called your mother. I told her that there had been an incident at the drop-in centre and that you'd been taken to the hospital to get checked out, but that there was nothing to worry about. The only reason she's not here right now is that I swore I would call her as soon as I found out what was going on."

"But, Dad — "

"And I promised to take you straight home. Give me a break, Robbie. If your mother found out that you'd had stitches and I hadn't told her, she'd skin me alive. Now come on." He helped me into my coat.

Ben was out in the hall. As he came toward me, he and my father exchanged looks. Then my father said, "I'm going to call your mother. I'll be right back."

"Nice going," Ben said after my father stepped outside with his cell phone. "Why didn't you just call the cops and have Mr. Duffy arrested? At least that way he'd have a nice, warm jail cell to spend the day in and a guaranteed hot meal."

"What are you talking about?" And why did he sound so angry with me all of a sudden?

"I talked to Mr. Donovan," he said. "He's going to bar Mr. Duffy from the drop-in centre for a week."

Oh.

"I didn't ask him to do that, Ben. He asked me if I wanted to press charges, and I said no. But Mr. Duffy *was* stealing. And because of him I had to get stitches. Just because he's homeless, that doesn't mean — "

"How would *you* like to be out in the cold for a whole week?" Ben said. "How would you like to have no place to go?" Before I could answer, he wheeled around and walked away. What was with him? He had been so nice to me when he saw I was hurt, but now he was acting like I had attacked Mr. Duffy instead of the other way around. Well, that was his problem. I went to look for my father.

* * *

My mother rushed out of the house as soon as my father's car pulled into her driveway. She turned pale when she saw the bandage on my face and the information sheet on head injuries that my father handed her.

"It's a *mild* concussion," my father and I said in unison. Then he said, "It sounds worse than it is. She's fine. Really." My mother glowered at him as though my injuries were his fault. She said, "You're not going back to that drop-in centre, do you understand me, Robyn?"

I told her not to worry, that I had no intention of going back. I'd had all I could take of Mr. Duffy — and of Ben Logan.

And of Nick. I wouldn't have been anywhere near the drop-in centre if it hadn't been for him. He still hadn't called. Where was he?

Chapter 4

That night, the temperature plummeted. The forecast called for another few days of severe cold. Billy called me on Monday night.

"How are you feeling, Robyn?" he said. He'd asked me the same question a dozen times at school that day. He said he knew Mr. Duffy, but that he had never known him to attack anyone before. He said he hoped I wasn't going to think that all homeless people did things like that, because it wasn't true.

"I'm still fine, Billy," I said. I had spent the whole day trying not to think about the possibility of a scar on my face.

"Mr. Donovan just called me," Billy said. "The city has issued a cold alert. When that happens, the drop-in centre operates twenty-four hours a day instead of closing overnight. I was wondering . . . "

"Don't even think about asking me, Billy," I said. I had promised myself on my way home from the hospital that I would never set foot in that drop-in centre again, no matter who asked me or what they said. Besides, even if I'd wanted to go, my mother would never let me.

"They're really short-handed, Robyn," Billy said. "Especially now. It's hard enough to get volunteers at night, especially on short notice. It's even worse so close to Christmas. And nothing will happen, I promise. We'll be working in groups. I'll make sure you're safe. Please? I wouldn't ask you if it wasn't important."

Now that I had actually been to the drop-in centre and knew what they did there and had seen some of the clients, it was so much easier to picture how much the place meant to the people who relied on it and so much harder to tell myself that it wasn't my problem. Still . . .

"I don't know, Billy . . . "

"They need people to help inside, and they need people in the vans."

"Vans?"

"They do patrols. They round up anyone who's sleeping outside, and they bring them in out of the cold. You would be in one of the vans with me. Come on, Robyn. It's really cold out there. This is the kind of night when people could literally freeze to death."

I pictured Andrew. I pictured the women with the bundle buggies who had been clustered around the TV.

"Well . . . "

"I'll meet you at the bus. We'll go together."

I hesitated.

"What about Morgan? Is she coming, too?" I said.

"She can't. She's got some family thing."

Family thing? She hadn't mentioned any family thing to me.

"So you'll come, right?" Billy said.

"Well . . . " If it were anyone else, I would have said no. But it was Billy, and Billy was so kind-hearted that he was making me feel like a grinch. Besides, I would be with him the whole time.

"I'll talk to my mom," I said. "I'll call you back."

My mother started shaking her head before I'd even finished explaining what I wanted to do.

"I thought we agreed you weren't going back there," she said.

"But Billy says they're short-handed."

"That may be, but after what happened the last time you were there — "

"I don't think that man meant to hurt me, Mom. Besides, he's been barred from the centre. He's probably at one of the shelters. Anyway, I'm not going alone. Billy's going to be with me."

My mother started to relent. Sure, she comes across like a mother lion when it comes to making sure I'm safe, but she isn't hard-hearted. And, like everyone else, she liked, trusted, and respected Billy.

"Billy said we might be late," I warned her.

"But it's a school night."

"I know. But I have a spare first thing in the morning. And, anyway, it's not like we're doing much. Most of my teachers are either doing review or they're giving us class time to finish projects and essays, and all of mine are done." Come Friday morning, we would be off school for a two-week Christmas break. "Come on, Mom. It's for a good cause. It's cold tonight. All I'm going to do is help people stay warm."

"What about you?" she said. "How are *you* going to stay warm? And how will you get home?"

"I'll be in a van," I said. When she still didn't look convinced, I added, "I'll bundle up. I promise. And when I'm finished, I'll hop a bus over to Dad's place. It's not that far from the centre." My father lived downtown. My mother lived uptown in a more sub-urban neighbourhood.

Eventually, after double-checking that I had packed extra mittens and making me promise that I would keep my hat on my head, my mother let me go.

* * *

Mr. Donovan came over and welcomed me when I arrived with Billy.

"This means a lot to us, Robyn," he said. "You can't believe how busy we get on a night like this."

I looked around and was surprised to see how many people were already bedding down on foam mattresses and fold-up cots.

"The regulars know that when it gets this cold, we'll be open for the night, so they show up on their own," Mr. Donovan said. "But there are a lot of other people out there who don't know or who need coaxing. We find them, tell them the centre is open, and bring them back here — if they want to come. We have a lot of territory to cover. I've assigned both of you to Eileen. Billy will introduce you, Robyn — I think Eileen's in the kitchen — and fill you in on what you'll be doing, okay, Billy?"

Billy had explained everything on our way to the centre. Some people, he said, prefer to sleep outside, no matter what. They don't like or can't tolerate the cramped quarters and noise of an emergency shelter or they're afraid someone will steal their few belongings. We would try to persuade everyone to come back to the centre, but we couldn't force them. Anyone who insisted on staying outside would be given hot soup and tea and an extra sleeping bag to get them through the night. Billy also told me that there was a team assigned to each of the centre's two vans — a professional social worker with enough medical training to know when a person either had to come in out of the cold or be transported to a hospital, and two volunteers whose job it was to hand out hot tea, hot soup, warm clothes, and sleeping bags. We headed for the kitchen.

As soon as Billy pushed open the kitchen door, I spotted Ben. He was loading cartons of soup into insulated boxes so that they would stay hot. Betty worked alongside him, filling thermos after thermos with sweet, milky tea. Another volunteer was packing boxes of foil-wrapped sandwiches. Ben looked up when we entered the room and greeted Billy warmly. He didn't say anything to me, and I didn't speak to him, either. Billy asked Betty where Eileen was. She nodded to the kitchen's rear door. We went out into the parking lot behind the church and found a young, thin, serious-looking woman, wearing a Tibetan-style hat with earflaps and the thickest pair of mittens I had ever seen, piling sleeping bags into the back of a van. Eileen. Billy introduced me and asked her what she needed us to do. She sent us back into the kitchen for soup and tea, which we loaded into the van.

"I think that's everything," Eileen said ten minutes later, her words turning into frosty white swirls in the frigid night air. "Let's get rolling."

The three of us climbed into the van. We had been assigned the west side of the downtown core. Eileen and Billy knew exactly where to look. We found people huddled under mounds of blankets and dirty old sleeping bags, on top of subway vents, in bus shelters, in dark alleys, and in the entrances to stores and office buildings. Every time we spotted someone, Eileen stopped the van, got out, and asked the person if he or she wanted a ride back to the drop-in centre. Mostly they were men, but there were a few women, some couples, and even two people with dogs.

If the person didn't want to leave his or her spot, we handed out the sleeping bags and warm food. Eileen made a note of where we had found the person and promised everyone who chose to stay on the street that someone would be back later that night to check on them. If people wanted to get in out of the cold, Eileen brought them back to the van, where we fed them, and then drove to the next spot on our route. When the van was full, we drove back to the centre.

Billy and I waited in the foyer while Eileen showed the passengers inside and helped to get them settled. A second van pulled up and Ben got out. I ignored him, and he made no move to speak to me, which suited me fine. When Eileen came out of the drop-in centre, we set off again.

The next three people we found refused transport back to the centre. Eileen tried to coax them. She warned them how cold it was going to get and what could happen to them if they stayed outside. When she had exhausted all of her arguments and they still didn't want transportation, she summoned me, and we made sure that each person had something warm to drink, something nourishing to eat, and a clean, new sleeping bag to help keep them warm. By midnight, we had given out almost everything we had, and had transported more than fifteen people back to the centre.

"I'd like to make one more run before we call it a night and hand it over to the next shift," Eileen said. "Is everyone okay with that?"

Billy and I nodded. I called my father and let him know what was going on.

"You're going to be tired tomorrow, Robbie," he said. "You'd better call me when you're done, and I'll come and get you."

We did one more circuit, each of us looking for the lumps of blankets and sleeping bags that marked another homeless person. For a long time, we saw no one. Then, "Up there," Eileen said, pointing to a bus shelter directly ahead of us.

"Over there," Billy said at almost exactly the same time, pointing to a figure lying in the doorway of an office building. Eileen stopped the van.

"I'll check the bus shelter," Eileen said. "You and Robyn go and check out that doorway."

Billy waited for me to join him, and we set off across the street to investigate the blanketed figure lying in the doorway.

The figure — I couldn't tell if it was a man or a woman — lay on top of a couple of old sleeping bags, covered only by one thin, worn blanket. Why, I wondered, on a night as cold as this, wouldn't the person have used the sleeping bags to cover up? I shivered as a gust of arctic air sent some old newspapers swirling. A paper cup and some fast-food wrappers scudded down the street. *Clink, clink, clink.* An empty bottle, propelled by the wind, rolled out of the alley next to the building and stopped at my feet. I glanced at it. It was a liquor bottle.

Billy was looking down at the figure.

"We'd better wake him up," he said. "It's the only way to make sure he's okay." He started to bend down.

"Wait!" I said, grabbing his arm.

He looked expectantly at me.

So far everyone we had approached had been awake or had at least stirred at our arrival. But not this person. This person seemed to be fast asleep. What would happen if Billy shook him — or her? What if he startled the person? Worse, what if whoever it was was delusional? Plenty of homeless people suffer from mental illness. Sometimes that's why they're homeless. Or sometimes they develop a mental illness because of their bleak situation. What if he shook the person, and the person responded by attacking him? My mind flashed back to my encounter with Mr. Duffy in the drop-in centre basement.

"I have to wake him up, Robyn," Billy said. "It'll be okay. I've done this before."

I stood back a few steps, just to be on the safe side, and watched him bend down and reach for what I assumed was a shoulder. He gave a gentle shake.

"Hello," he said. "Hello."

No response.

I edged in close to Billy. The person hadn't moved. Billy pulled the blanket down a little so that he could see who he was shaking. It was a man with a scruffy beard. He was lying on his side with his face pressed in against the door. Billy shook him again, more vigorously this time. The man fell over onto his back. It was Mr. Duffy. But his eyes were still closed

Billy glanced at me. Then he shook him again, even harder.

"Mr. Duffy," he said. "Wake up, Mr. Duffy. We've got a hot drink for you."

There was something funny about the way he was lying. He seemed so still. Too still. Little clouds of white plumed from Billy's and my nose and mouth, but not from Mr. Duffy. I crouched down beside Billy, no longer afraid that Mr. Duffy would lash out at me, and loosened the scarf, stiff with grease and grit, that was wound around his neck. Billy looked

53

bleakly at me as I pulled my mitten off and gingerly pressed my fingers against the side of his neck to check for a pulse.

I glanced at Billy. "You'd better get Eileen," I said.

* * *

Eileen did the same thing I had done — she felt for a pulse. Then she fished out a cell phone, called 911, and asked them to send an ambulance.

"Is he — " Billy began.

"I'm not a doctor," Eileen said, her face grim. "So I have to call 911. It's procedure."

Eileen urged us to go back to the van to wait, but I couldn't make myself go. I kept checking my watch. I wished the paramedics would hurry up. Maybe it wasn't hopeless. Maybe there was something they could do.

Finally the paramedics arrived. So did a police cruiser. After the paramedics had examined Mr. Duffy and had been in contact with a hospital, Mr. Duffy was pronounced dead. The police called the coroner. Billy turned and walked back to the van. He sat there, his head bowed slightly, until Eileen went to get him again so that the police could talk to him. They talked to each one of us alone. They asked me to tell them everything I knew about Mr. Duffy. It didn't amount to much. They asked me twice exactly when we had spotted him, what we had done when we approached him, what we had touched, and where exactly we had stepped. They asked Billy the same questions.

"What happens now?" I heard him ask one of the police officers.

"The coroner will probably order an autopsy," the officer said, "to determine cause of death. Me, I'm hoping for natural causes — maybe he had a pre-existing medical condition or maybe it was a heart attack. I'd hate to think the poor guy froze to death." He gave us a sympathetic look as he closed his note-book. "What you kids are doing is great. If there were more people like you around, the world would be a better place."

"If there was more affordable housing and more help available for people like Mr. Duffy, then you wouldn't need people like us," Eileen said.

The cop didn't argue.

By the time the police left, it was nearly two in the morning. On our way back to the drop-in centre, I got out my cell phone and called my father.

"Robbie, I was just about to call you," he said. "I was getting worried." When I told him what had happened, he said, "You and Billy stay put. I'll be there as soon as I can."

When we got back to the drop-in centre, everyone seemed to know what had happened. Eileen and Mr. Donovan huddled together in the foyer. I saw Billy talking to Ben. Ben glanced at me, a grim expression on his face. My stomach clenched when he and Billy walked toward me.

"I still can't believe it," Billy said. "Mr. Duffy was practically the first person I met when I started vol-unteering at this drop-in centre. I saw him almost every time I came down here."

Ben looked sharply at me. "If you hadn't said anything to Mr. Donovan, Mr. Duffy wouldn't have been barred from the drop-in centre. He would have showed up on his own when the temperature dropped. We wouldn't have had to go looking for him. For sure you wouldn't have found him dead."

I stared at him, stung. Was he right? Was I responsible?

"Hey," Billy said. "It's not Robyn's fault. We don't even know how he died. Maybe it's like the police said. Maybe it was natural causes. Or maybe there was something else wrong with him. You know as well as I do that people who live on the street develop all kinds of health problems."

I sure hoped that Billy was right.

"Sure," Ben said. "It's the coldest night of the year — so cold that the city issues a cold alert — and we find him dead under one thin blanket. It was definitely natural causes."

"He could have gone someplace else," I said. "There are plenty of shelters — "

"He didn't feel comfortable in most of those places," Ben said. "But he liked the drop-in centre. He felt safe here. I told Mr. Donovan that."

That was news to me.

A sleek, black Porsche pulled up outside. Its horn tooted and I raised a hand to wave. Ben arched an eyebrow as he looked from the car to me. I felt his eyes on me, but I refused to look at him. I grabbed Billy's hand, and we ran down the steps and got into my father's car.

Chapter 5

The next day, when Morgan and I were on our way out of school, she suddenly elbowed me in the ribs.

"Look who's here," she said, grinning at me. She pointed down the stairs. Ben was leaning against the wall just inside the main doors. "He's really cute, Robyn. You two would look great together."

"He hates me, Morgan. He practically accused me of killing a homeless person."

"I know. But that's ridiculous," she said. "He probably came to apologize." She waved at him. "Hi, Ben."

Ben nodded in acknowledgement, but he kept his eyes on me. Morgan jabbed me with her elbow again.

"If I end up with a bruise, you're going to be sorry, Morgan."

"Look at the way he's looking at you," she whispered. "He's definitely interested. I can tell." She flashed me another grin, said, "I have to run," and retreated to a bank of lockers down the hall, where she pretended to busy herself with a lock that wasn't hers.

Ben stood where he was. He stared at me but didn't say a word.

"What's the matter?" I said. The way he was looking at me was giving me the creeps.

"Mr. Duffy didn't die of natural causes. It wasn't a heart attack or a stroke or anything like that."

If you'd just glanced at him, you would have thought he was perfectly calm. You had to look closely to see that he was trembling all over and that what looked like calmness was the effort he was making to keep all that trembling under control. I started to get a bad feeling.

"What did he die of?" I said, even though I was pretty sure I already knew the answer.

"He froze to death."

I felt sick inside.

"That's awful," I said. "I'm sorry."

"You should be." He was blaming me. He was definitely blaming me.

"I'm sure everyone who knew him is sorry, Ben."

"Right," he said. "But it's not *everyone's* fault that he died the way he did. If you hadn't ratted him out to Mr. Donovan — "

"I'm sorry," I said again. "But I was upset. He scared me. I was bleeding." I touched the ugly bandage on the right side of my face. "I told Mr. Donovan that I didn't think he meant to hurt me. I never meant for anything to happen to him."

"I wish you'd never come down to the drop-in

centre," Ben said. "Then this never would have happened."

"I'm sorry," I said. "I'm really sorry."

Ben glared at me a moment longer before turning and stalking out of the school.

Morgan came back to join me. "I guess that didn't go so well, huh?" she said.

* * *

"Do you think I did the wrong thing?" I asked my father when I got to his place after school.

He looked surprised.

"Why?" he said. "Do *you*?"

"Well, he *was* homeless," I said.

"That's hardly your fault, Robbie."

"But if I hadn't told Mr. Donovan what happened —"

"I know how you must feel," my father said. "It's a real tragedy that he froze to death. It's a tragedy that anyone freezes to death in this day and age, especially in a big city like this. But it sounds to me as if he had other problems besides being homeless."

"I know," I said. But I couldn't stop thinking about what Ben had said and the way he had looked at me. "But if he hadn't been barred from the drop-in centre, he might still be alive."

"If he hadn't become aggressive with you, he probably would have become aggressive with someone else. If it had been another volunteer in the kitchen when he snuck down into the basement, even if it had been a staff member, he probably would have acted the same way he did with you. You're lucky you weren't badly hurt, Robbie. And it could just as easily have been someone else."

"If it *had* been someone else, they might have handled it better than I did."

My father looked at me for a few moments. "I could think of a hundred ifs, Robbie," he said. "But it is what it is. All you did was answer Mr. Donovan's questions truthfully. After that, it was out of your hands. You had no way of knowing what he was going to do. And you certainly had no way of knowing that this man would sleep outside on the coldest night of the year instead of making his way to an emergency shelter. As I understand it, he had been homeless for quite some time. He must have known all the local shelters. He must have known there were other places to go."

I knew my father was trying to make me feel better. I even knew that most of what he was saying was true. But it didn't help. I felt terrible.

* * *

"It's terrible that that old guy froze to death," Morgan said when I called her later. "But it's not exactly a first. It happens every year."

"I know. But everyone thinks it's my fault."

"*Everyone?*"

"Well, Ben does. And I wouldn't be surprised if Billy did, too."

There was silence on the other end of the phone. Terrific.

"He does, doesn't he, Morgan? Billy blames me."

"Billy's a non-judgmental person, Robyn."

That was true. "But there's no way he would ever rat on a homeless person," I said.

"Come on, Robyn, you know Billy. He would probably have given the guy every cent he had to go and buy food if he thought he was hungry enough to steal. But for what it's worth, if it had been me, I would have pressed charges."

I love Morgan. She's my best friend. But somehow what she said didn't make me feel better.

"I gotta go," I said. "I have to call Billy. I need Ben's phone number."

* * *

When Ben agreed to meet me, he was about as enthusiastic as a person booking an appointment for major dental surgery. When I sat down opposite him after supper that night in a coffee shop he had chosen, he gave me a sour look.

"It was on the news," he said. "Did you see it?" I hadn't. *"Homeless man freezes to death. First one this winter."* He sounded angry. "Do you know how many homeless people froze to death *last* winter?" He looked disgusted when I said I didn't. "Four. The winter before that it was three. But nobody cares."

"I wouldn't say that — "

"You know what the worst part is? The worst part is that no one even knows who he is — I mean, who he was."

"What do you mean?"

"All anyone knows about Mr. Duffy is his name, and no one's even positive that Duffy was his real name."

61

"Come on," I said. "People must know more than that about him. Someone must know who he is and where he came from. He must have had some identification."

Ben shook his head. "Mr. Donovan said the police couldn't find any. All he had on him when he died was a couple of paperback novels, a wad of paper napkins, and some ketchup packets. The police asked around, but no one knows anything about him. They don't know where he came from or how he ended up on the street. No one even knows his first name. Mr. Donovan says they fingerprinted him at the morgue to see if they could identify him that way. But they couldn't. You know what that means? It means he'll end up getting a cheap funeral at city expense. He won't even get a real headstone. But what's the point, huh? They wouldn't even know what name to put on it. He'll just be one more pathetic, anonymous homeless man who drank too much and froze to death."

"Drank too much?"

"That's what they said on the news. He'd been drinking. They think he passed out and that's why he froze to death."

"Oh," I said. I thought about the liquor bottle I had seen on the sidewalk near where we had found Mr. Duffy.

Ben's eyes zeroed right in on me. "What does that mean — 'Oh'?"

"Nothing," I said quickly.

"I know what you're thinking," Ben said. "When people see homeless guys like Mr. Duffy having a drink or smoking a cigarette, they think they're committing some kind of crime. They think if homeless people didn't smoke or drink, they'd probably be able to afford food, or a place to stay. Well, it doesn't work that way. They're on the street because they're sick or because they've hit bottom and they can't get back up again. Sometimes a smoke or a drink is the only pleasure they have in life. It's not a crime. And, anyway, Mr. Duffy was trying to quit. Mr. Donovan told me." Too bad he hadn't succeeded, I thought. Ben shook his head impatiently. "When I heard you were Billy's friend, I thought maybe I'd been wrong about you. But I guess I wasn't. When it comes right down to it, you don't see someone like Mr. Duffy as a real person who deserves the same things in life that you have."

"That's not true," I said. "I called you because I feel terrible about what happened and because I want to know if there's anything I can do. Anything at all."

"Right," he said.

"I mean it, Ben."

He looked critically at me for a few moments. "Really?" he said. "Anything?"

* * *

I arrived back at my father's loft just in time to see my father's (young) friend Tara leave the building and climb into a taxi. I wondered how she figured into my father's life. The whole time my parents were separated, my father acted as if he thought they would eventually get back together. They never did. He had seemed stunned when my mother finally divorced him. But as far as I knew, he hadn't yet become seriously involved with another woman. My mother, on the other hand, was seeing Ted Gold — he had recently proposed to her. My mother hadn't said yes, but she hadn't said no, either, and it seemed to me that she and Ted were closer than ever. Had my father finally got the hint? Had he finally decided to move on?

I found him sitting on a stool in his kitchen, sipping coffee and reading the newspaper. He glanced up when I came through the door.

"Robbie," he said. "Where did you disappear to?"

"I had to meet someone."

"I've got something for you," he said. He slid off his stool, went into the living room, and picked up some papers that were lying on the coffee table. He handed them to me.

I scanned the top page. *Autopsy report,* it said. *Last name: Duffy. First name: Unknown. DOB: Unknown. Age: Approximately 60–65.*

"Where did you get this, Dad?"

"From the pathologist. She faxed this over to me — at my request."

"She?"

My father grinned. "A very pretty she," he said. He took the report from me. "Basically what it says is that your Mr. Duffy was in poor health." He ran a finger down the page. "At some point in the past, he suffered a serious head trauma, which may at least partly explain why he was on the street. He also suffered damage to his face. Serena says he must have had poor vision in his left eye."

"Serena?"

"The pathologist. And — the big one, Robbie — the man ingested a *lot* of alcohol just before he died."

"I already know that, Dad."

"You do?"

"Ben told me."

"Maybe someone treated him to some pre-Christmas cheer. Or maybe he collected enough panhandling to buy himself a bottle. Some people think that alcohol will warm them up on a cold night. They don't realize the risks it poses."

"Is that supposed to make me feel better? Because it's having the opposite effect."

"What I'm saying is, if he drank as much as Serena says he did, then he probably passed out. And that could just as easily have happened even if he hadn't been barred from the drop-in centre. You drink that much, Robbie, and you don't think straight. You don't do the sensible thing. You did tell me that he was lying *on top* of a couple of sleeping bags, didn't you? He wasn't in them or covered by them. That suggests to me that he passed out before he could take even the most basic precautions against the cold. It's not your fault, Robbie. Chances are what happened would have happened no matter what."

Maybe he was right. But I still couldn't shake the feeling that Ben had a point. If I hadn't said anything to Mr. Donovan, the night might have turned out differently for Mr. Duffy. He might have stayed at the drop-in centre. He might not have tried to warm himself up with alcohol. He might still be alive.

"Nobody knows anything about him, Dad. According to Ben, no one even knows if Duffy was his real name. They don't know what happened to him or if he had any family. Ben says he's going to be buried at city expense. That bothers him."

"At least he gets a funeral and a burial," my father said.

"But no full name to go with it. Ben says that Mr. Duffy didn't have any identification on him — no birth certificate, no health card, no social insurance card. No passport. No bank card. No old letters or bills. Not even a library card. How can that be, Dad? Everyone has some kind of identification."

My father shrugged. "Maybe he lost whatever he had. Maybe it got stolen. Or maybe he stashed any valuables he had in a safe place so they wouldn't get stolen. It can be rough on the street."

"The thing is, Ben wants to do something for Mr. Duffy. He doesn't want him to be just one more anonymous homeless person who froze to death. He wants to find out more about him so that he can hold a memorial service for him." Ben had been so earnest when he'd told me what he wanted to do. He had also been sure that I wouldn't care. But I did. Okay, so maybe guilt had a lot to do with why I'd offered to help. But the more I thought about it, the more it seemed like the right thing to do

My father arched an eyebrow. "You seem to care an awful lot about what this Ben thinks."

Yeah, right. That would be the day.

"It's not about Ben. It's about Mr. Duffy. I want to do something. But I don't know where to start. The police tried to identify Mr. Duffy by his fingerprints, but they struck out."

"All that means is that the man didn't have a criminal record."

I thought back to my experience with Mr. Duffy. He had been so aggressive that I found it difficult to believe he'd never been in trouble with the law.

"What about dental records?" I said. "Can't they use those?"

"Dental records are only useful if you have some idea who the person is," my father said. "Otherwise, how do you know which of literally thousands of dentists in the city to check with? And that's assuming that Mr. Duffy was from here originally or, if he wasn't, that he had dental work done while he lived here — which, based on Serena's report, seems doubtful."

"But someone must have some kind of record of him, right?"

The answer I wanted was: "Yes." The answer I got was: "Not necessarily."

"Great. So basically I volunteered for Mission Impossible."

"Why do you say that?"

"Because if the police can't find out — "

"The man froze to death, Robbie. As far as the police are concerned, his death was an accident, not the result of a criminal act. They did what they could to find out who he was, but it's not a high priority if no crime was committed. But Mission Impossible? I wouldn't jump to that conclusion."

"You mean there is some way we can find out who he was?"

"I wouldn't necessarily say that, either."

"Then what *would* you say?"

"If it were me, Robbie, if someone hired me to find out who he was, you know what I'd do?"

I shook my head.

"I'd talk to people."

"But Ben said — "

"The man lived in this city. He interacted with people. He was a regular at the drop-in centre and probably at other homeless shelters or soup kitchens around town."

"But if no one at the drop-in centre knows anything about him — "

"Oh?" my father said. "You spoke to all the staff and all the regulars there?"

"Well, no, but — "

"One person might know one little thing. Another person might know something else."

"So I should talk to people at the centre?"

"It would be a start. You could also check out Mr. Duffy's territory."

"His territory?"

"Panhandlers usually stake out a spot that they consider their own. They're there day after day. And there are bound to be people who pass that same spot every day, maybe on their way to and from work. Some of them may have dropped money into Mr.

Duffy's hat. Some people make a habit of it, Robbie — a loonie or toonie every day."

"You think that some of them might have talked to Mr. Duffy?"

"It's worth a shot. Another thing, Robbie. Just because Mr. Duffy didn't have a regular place to stay, that doesn't mean he wasn't in contact with people — a lot of people. For example, he had to get his clothes from somewhere."

"Maybe from second-hand stores or charity thrift shops," I said.

My father grinned. "And I doubt he spent all his spare time at the drop-in centre," he said. "If he was panhandling, then he probably had some cash at least some of the time, and he probably spent it on food or drink, and maybe on toiletries."

"I could check with some of the stores and restaurants in the area," I said. This was beginning to sound like a big job.

"Did he have anything on him when they found him?" my father said. "Did he carry anything with him? Some homeless people drag their belongings around in a bag or a bundle buggy."

I thought back to the night we had found Mr. Duffy and to what Ben had told me in the coffee shop. "All I saw were those sleeping bags and that old blanket," I said. "I don't remember any bags or a bundle buggy. Ben said that Mr. Donovan told him that all Mr. Duffy had with him were a couple of paperback novels, some paper napkins, and some ketchup packets."

"What about a liquor bottle?"

I had to think for a moment. "There was a bottle rolling around near him," I said at last.

"You remember what it was?"

"Sure. That Napoleon stuff you and Vern like to drink."

"Cognac?" my father said. He sounded surprised. "Doesn't sound like something a homeless person would be able to afford. But I guess you never know."

"Maybe that wasn't his bottle."

"You're probably right," my father said. "Those books, though, they could be interesting."

"You mean, I could check out where he got them?"

"Or if there's anything tucked inside."

"What about those napkins and the ketchup packets?" I said. "Maybe they have a logo on them."

My father looked positively proud of me. "Good thinking, Robbie. Also, where did he hang out when he wasn't at the drop-in centre? In a park? A library?"

"Or an underground parking garage. Billy says lots of homeless people sneak into parking garages to get warm."

"Is there a walk-in clinic in the area?"

"I can check." But I was definitely going to need help. "Sounds like you do this a lot, Dad."

"Well, I don't know about a lot. But, sometimes."

I looked at him with new respect. "You like it?"

He grinned. "I like puzzles, Robbie. That's what this is. A gigantic puzzle. But before you can begin to solve it, you have to hunt for the puzzle pieces." His face grew more serious.

"What?" I said. "Is something wrong?"

He hesitated.

"I ran into Ed Jarvis today," he said finally. Ed Jarvis had been Nick's probation officer.

My heart started to race. "Does he know where Nick is? Is he okay?"

"He didn't even know that Nick was gone."

Oh.

"So he hasn't talked to him? He has no idea where he is?"

It looked like my father was going to say something, but he hesitated again.

"What?" I said. "What did he say?"

"Only that it's possible that Nick got into trouble again and that's why he took off. He says he's seen it happen before — kids like Nick straighten out for a while and then they mess up. And when they do, they sometimes go out of their way to avoid the people who have helped them. They're ashamed of themselves for slipping and they're afraid they've disappointed the people who care for them."

"You don't think Nick — "

"I don't know what to think, Robbie. I'm just telling you what Ed said, and he knows Nick a lot better than I do."

I struggled to keep back my tears. I missed Nick. I was worried about him. I wished I knew where he was. But I didn't, and until he contacted me, there was nothing I could do.

Chapter 6

"I hate this," Morgan said at eleven-thirty the next day. We had a double lunch period followed by gym, which had morphed into library time because our phys. ed. teacher was out sick. Morgan had been ecstatic when she'd heard that. She'd wanted to spend the extra time doing Christmas shopping. Instead I had convinced her to come down to the drop-in centre with me so that she could help me talk to people. I had asked Billy, too — the more, the easier? — but he had a review lab he couldn't miss.

"How can you hate it?" I said. "We haven't even started yet."

In fact, we had just got off the bus. Morgan was clutching a giant cup of latte, which she had insisted she needed to "keep her going."

"I mean, I hate that it's so dirty and depressing down here," she said, shivering inside her faux-fur coat as she glanced up and down the street.

It had snowed about a week ago, which had made

some neighbourhoods, like my mother's, look like a scene from a Christmas card — rolling, snow-covered lawns; white, snow-covered pine trees; all that snow reflecting the glow of Christmas lights. But, boy, not this neighbourhood. In this neighbourhood, a layer of grime and litter had settled on the once-pristine snow. It was not a festive sight.

"I bet you don't complain when you're down here with Billy," I said.

She shook her head. "If I did, Billy would take it as a criticism of poor people." She sighed. "He's so sweet. I adore him, really I do. But he doesn't think poor people can be held responsible if their neighbourhoods are dirty and depressing. But, come on, it doesn't cost anything to pick up after yourself. Am I right or am I right?" She gulped down the last mouthful of her latte and looked around for a garbage can. There were none in sight. "Oh," she said. She held onto the cardboard coffee container, if only to prove her point. "So, now what?"

"Now we start talking to people. We might as well begin in the obvious place." I nodded down the street toward the drop-in centre. A knot of smokers had gathered in a circle outside the main door. Morgan looked apprehensively at them.

"What if they won't talk to us?"

"If they won't, they won't."

"What if some of them are, you know . . . " I waited, pretending I didn't know. "You know," she said again. "What if some of them are a little crazy?"

"You've spent more time here than I have, Morgan.

Why are you acting like you're afraid of these people?"

"You're telling me you're not?"

"They're homeless. They're not criminals."

"Then why did you beg me to come with you? Why didn't you come down here alone? Or, better yet, if this is so important to Ben, why isn't he here with you instead of me? It would give you two a chance to become better acquainted. Billy says he's nice when you get to know him. And he's really hot, Robyn."

"First of all, I offered to do this. Me. Not him. Second, I'm *not* interested in him."

"But with Nick gone — "

"I don't want to talk about Nick. I just want to do what I said I'd do. I asked you to come with me because you're my best friend. We have to talk to *a lot* of people. Two people can cover twice as much territory."

"Right." She did not sound convinced and trailed half a step behind me as we walked the rest of the way to the drop-in centre. When we got there, the smokers ignored us.

"Excuse me," I said.

They continued to ignore us. I moved closer to the small circle and tapped one of the smokers on the arm.

"Excuse me, sir."

He turned. So did everyone else. He was about my height, with stubble all over his cheeks and chin, and a cap with earflaps that he had pulled down low on his forehead. He glowered at me from beneath the visor. His mismatched eyes — the left one was dark, but the right one was cloudy white — made him look particularly sinister. He was smoking what looked like a hand-rolled cigarette, which he held with cold-reddened fingers that poked out from the unravelling ends of dingy grey woollen gloves.

"Hi," I said again, trying not to stare at the milky eye. The man made no response. "I was wondering if I could ask you — all of you — a few questions about Mr. Duffy."

It was already cold outside, but it suddenly got a lot colder. Half of the smokers shifted their eyes to the ground. A couple shuffled down the sidewalk, away from Morgan and me. A couple of others, including the man with the mismatched eyes, stared hard at me. No one said a word. I wondered if they knew that I had ratted on Mr. Duffy. If they did, I wondered what they thought of me. Morgan tugged on my elbow, but I held my ground.

"I'm helping Ben," I said. "You know Ben?" Nothing. Not a nod, not a glint of acknowledgement in anyone's eye, certainly not a friendly smile. "Ben wants to hold a memorial service for Mr. Duffy. He asked me to help him by talking to people who knew Mr. Duffy, so that he can say something about Mr. Duffy at the service."

The two men who had been looking at me now looked away. The men who hadn't already left now moved down the street, away from the drop-in centre and the two uptown girls who were asking questions.

"Well, we're off to a good start," Morgan said, watching them. "What do you say we go inside where we can at least be warm while we're being ignored?"

It was the first good idea Morgan had had all morning.

* * *

"Why don't we talk to whoever is in charge around here?" Morgan said. She glanced around the interior of the drop-in centre, spotted a garbage can, and rid herself of her giant latte cup. "I bet they know something."

Mr. Donovan spotted me and came over to us. "Ben told me what you're doing," he said after we had explained why we were there. "I wish I could help. But Mr. Duffy never said much to me. In fact, he seemed to go out of his way to avoid talking to me."

"You must have some kind of records, some kind of information on him," Morgan said. "Ben said he was here all the time."

Mr. Donovan smiled pleasantly at her. "It's Megan, isn't it?" he said, which surprised me. Mr. Donovan struck me as someone who was good with names.

"Actually, it's Morgan," Morgan said.

"Morgan," Mr. Donovan said, as if he were trying out the name. "Sorry. You're right about Mr. Duffy being here a lot. But I'm afraid we don't have any records. Not on Mr. Duffy, anyway. Not on most of the people who use the centre, for that matter. Our mandate is to offer a safe place for the homeless to get out of the cold — or, in summer, out of the heat —

provide them with something to eat, and help them get whatever services they might need: medical, social, or employment services. Anything they may require and will agree to."

"Did Mr. Duffy use any services?" I said.

"Not that I know of. He was pretty independent. He never made any trouble, either." When I looked sceptical, he said, "Well, up until about six months ago. Mostly, Mr. Duffy was quiet and kept to himself. It's only recently that he started acting up. Maybe he said something to Betty. She chased him out of the kitchen often enough."

"Who's Betty?" Morgan asked after Mr. Donovan had left.

I sighed. It was just like Morgan to volunteer somewhere and not remember the names of staff and other volunteers.

"She's the cook," I said.

"Great. Let's go and talk to her." She grabbed my hand and started to drag me across the room.

"The kitchen's *that* way," I said, pointing in the opposite direction.

When we got to the kitchen door, Morgan nudged me in ahead of her. "This is your project," she said. "You ask."

I sighed and led the way inside.

"What do I know about Mr. Duffy?" Betty said after I had told her why we were there. She thought for a moment and shrugged. "Not much, I'm afraid. Except that he liked my beef and barley soup. He always asked for seconds."

"He never told you anything about his life?"

"Not a thing."

"Did you even ask?" Morgan said, sounding exasperated, as if it were Betty's job to at least know *something*.

"Well, I didn't pry, if that's what you mean," Betty said a little stiffly. "A lot of the people who come here don't want to talk about their past lives. It's too painful for them to think about the times when things were better or, for some of them, when they were worse. Some people end up on the street because of tragedy or misfortune — they get sick or they lose their jobs or families. Other people run to the street because it's better than whatever they used to call home. Either way, once they hit bottom, it's hard for them to pick themselves up again. So a lot of them don't appreciate being quizzed about their personal lives any more than anyone else does. If they tell me something, fine. But I don't go around asking. And with Mr. Duffy — well, he never volunteered anything."

"What about the food he stole?" Morgan said.

I blushed. I didn't want Betty to think that I'd been speaking ill of Mr. Duffy. But Betty just shook her head sadly.

"He particularly liked to stock up on cookies," she said. Then she frowned. "He never used to be one for desserts. He must have developed a sweet tooth."

I thanked her for her time.

"This will go faster if we split up," I told Morgan. "I'll talk to the people who are eating breakfast and you talk to the people who are watching TV." She looked apprehensively at the half dozen or so people who were camped out around the television. She didn't move. "They're just people," I said, trying to convince myself as much as her. What if they looked at me the way Ben did — as a two-four who dropped by once or twice and then vanished? What if one — or more — of them was just like Mr. Duffy? But we were here, and I had promised. "Some of them, if not most of them, knew Mr. Duffy. I bet they'll want to help us."

Morgan looked doubtful.

We split up. Twenty minutes later, we regrouped.

"Well, that was fun," Morgan said, clearly disgruntled. "How did you make out?"

"Not great," I said. "In fact, except for that man at the end of the table, no one would even talk to me." I nodded to an old man who was wearing not one, but two, overcoats and who was glistening with sweat as a result. "But he didn't want to talk about Mr. Duffy. He wanted to talk about how someone took his stuff last winter." He had told me that was why he always wore all of his clothes at the same time — so that no one could steal them. "What about you? Did you find out anything?"

Morgan shook her head in disgust. "Nobody knows anything — not his first name or where he came from or how he ended up on the street. Or, if they *do* know, they're not telling." She looked pointedly at me. "If Ben's relying on my information, pretty much all he'll be able to say is that Mr. Duffy quit drinking for good before he died."

Quit drinking for good?

"What are you talking about, Morgan?"

She gave me an exasperated look.

"Am I suddenly speaking Urdu or something? Someone told me that Mr. Duffy quit drinking for good a few months ago."

"Morgan, he died because he passed out after drinking too much."

"I'm aware of that," Morgan said, annoyed now that I was challenging her. "I'm just telling you what a woman told me. She was quite definite about it, Robyn. She said that he'd quit drinking. She thinks the police are lying about how he died — that they're saying he was drinking because they're trying to blame him when the real reason he died is that he was barred — " She broke off suddenly. "Sorry," she muttered. "That's what she said. I — "

"Who told you that, Morgan?"

"The woman in front of the TV." She turned to point. "Oh," she said, deflating a little. "She was there a minute ago."

"What was her name?"

"I didn't ask. Look, Robyn, I'm sure she just — "

"It sounds like she might have known Mr. Duffy pretty well," I said. "Maybe she knows something else about him. Maybe he talked to her. What did she look like?"

"Like a bag lady. Middle-aged. She was wearing a *lot* of clothes. And she had a bundle buggy parked beside her chair."

"You mean Aggie," said a voice behind me. I turned toward it.

"It's Andrew, right?" I said.

He seemed pleased that I knew his name. He peered at the bandage that was only half hidden by my hair. "Are you okay?"

"I had to get a couple of stitches," I said. "But I'm fine." Still, now that he'd reminded me, I couldn't help fingering the bandage and wondering again about the possibility of a scar.

"I heard you asking about Mr. Duffy," he said. He had a funny, mumbly way of talking. His lips hardly moved, and he kept his head bowed a little so that, even though he was taller than me, he seemed to be looking up at me while he spoke.

"Do you know anything about him, Andrew?"

He shook his head. "He never talked to me. He didn't talk much to anyone here. I seen him with Aggie a couple of times, though."

"Do you know where we can find her?"

He shook his head again. "But she'll be back. She always comes back."

"Do you know where Mr. Duffy spent his time when he wasn't here?"

"He liked an office building over on Victoria Street," Andrew said. "It was his place. He did pretty good there, too, considering how he treated some people."

"What do you mean?" Morgan said.

"He yelled at them sometimes."

I knew what he meant. I remembered how Mr.

Duffy had cursed at the man who had dropped a five-dollar bill into his hat.

"I seen him do it a couple of days ago," Andrew said, looking shyly at Morgan. "A man was trying to give him something — "

"You mean, money?" I said.

"I don't know. I guess. He was holding something out to Mr. Duffy, and Mr. Duffy was yelling at him. He was all huddled over, you know, like maybe he just wanted the man to go away or something. It was weird, but Mr. Duffy is like that sometimes. If some guy was trying to give me money — if *anyone* was trying to give *me* money — you'd better believe I'd take it."

"Where was this?" I asked.

"Same place," he said. "In front of that office building." He peered at me. "Why are you asking so many questions about him?"

"Because Ben wants to hold a memorial service for him and I'm trying to help," I said.

He thought about that for a moment. "If I hear anything," he said, "I'll let you know."

I watched him make his way to the door and wondered what had brought him to the street.

Morgan and I were on our way out of the drop-in centre when Mr. Donovan called my name.

"I have something for you," he said. He handed me a photograph. It was a group shot of what looked liked clients of the drop-in centre. "That's Mr. Duffy," he said, pointing to the man on the far left. "It's not the greatest picture in the world, but it's the only one

I could find of him. You can have it if you want."

"Okay, that's that," Morgan said, cheerful now that we were out on the street again. "Let's go shopping."

"Not yet."

"Aw, come on, Robyn. There are only nine more shopping days left."

"You said you'd help me, Morgan."

"Excuse me, but what was I just doing?"

I gave her a look.

"Okay, okay," she grumbled. "What do you want me to do?"

Chapter 7

"Now can we go home?" Morgan said a few hours later. "My feet are killing me. I'm cold. And I still have spit on the front of my coat. That stuff sticks like glue. What if that woman — "

"Aggie. Her name is Aggie."

"What if *Aggie* has a communicable disease? A lot of those people do, you know."

"Why are you acting so squeamish today? You volunteer at the drop-in centre."

Morgan's cheeks, already red from the cold, got a little redder.

"You *do* volunteer there, don't you, Morgan?"

"I'd like to," she said. "I know it's important to Billy. But you know how unpredictable my schedule can be."

Hmmmm.

"So exactly how many times *have* you been down here?" I said.

"Come on, Robyn. If I came down here every single

time Billy asked me to, I'd never have any time for myself."

"How many times?"

"I was here once at the beginning of November."

"For how long?"

"What difference does it make?"

Was it my imagination, or did she sound defensive?

"For how long, Morgan?"

She shrugged and looked down at the sidewalk. "A couple of hours."

"A couple of *hours?*"

"I had a hair appointment. I dropped by to pick up Billy when I was finished, and I helped him sort out some clothing donations."

"And since then?"

"Well . . ."

That explained why Mr. Donovan hadn't remembered her name. I should have known. Morgan was my best friend. She was madly in love with Billy, even though she and he were polar opposites. But she was *not* a people person, especially not a homeless people person.

"I thought volunteering to help live people would be better than volunteering to pick up dead birds," she said. During the last migration season, Morgan had spent a day sorting through dead birds collected by the Downtown Avian Rescue Club. She had spent the whole of the following week complaining about the stench of death that, she said, had clung to her hair and her skin, even though she'd smelled perfectly normal to me. "It turns out I was wrong."

"Sooner or later Billy is going to expect you to actually show up," I said.

"Maybe by then he'll be involved in something else. You know, maybe something I can handle."

Uh-huh.

"Robyn, can we *please* go somewhere warm?"

I looked up and down the street. The only possibility I saw was a place called Sal's Open Kitchen. It looked decidedly down-market. I glanced sceptically at Morgan.

A gust of icy wind caught us both, and we shivered.

"I can hardly feel my fingers and toes," she said. "And my face feels numb. I could be drooling and not even know it. If Sal's is heated, that's good enough for me." She changed her mind as soon as she pushed open the door and looked around. "On second thought, maybe we should go someplace else."

"The closest someplace else is at least five blocks that way," I said, pointing.

"But that's *into* the wind," Morgan said. She took another look at Sal's long, narrow interior. One side was taken up by a counter that ran the length of the place. Three of its stools were occupied. Half a dozen four-person tables filled the other half of the room. A couple of the tables at the rear were occupied — by men drinking beer. "Maybe if we sit up front." She headed for the table closest to the window and inspected a scarred, vinyl-covered chair closely before dropping down onto it. She unbuttoned her coat and removed it gingerly. "I'm going to have to have it dry cleaned," she said. "I still can't believe she spat at me."

"I guess she doesn't like to be called a liar," I said. Morgan had spotted Aggie, the woman she had talked to at the drop-in centre, just as we were dividing up the places that we needed to visit.

"Well I guess *not*," Morgan said. "But why did she spit at *me*? You're the one who made her angry."

Morgan had dragged me over to where Aggie was standing, rooting through some trash cans in an alley alongside a variety store, and had demanded, as only Morgan can, that Aggie repeat what she'd said earlier about Mr. Duffy. At first, Aggie didn't want to talk, so Morgan had fished in her pocket and surrendered all of her spare change. Then, when Aggie repeated what she had already told Morgan, Morgan looked triumphantly at me. When I (stupidly) told Aggie what everyone from Ben to Mr. Donovan to Serena the pathologist and my father had said — that Mr. Duffy couldn't exactly have quit for good because he had passed out from drinking too much — Aggie had flown into a rage. That's when she'd spat at Morgan.

"I think she was aiming at me," I said, "if it's any consolation."

"It isn't," Morgan said.

A sad-looking man in a grease-spattered, once-white apron shuffled over to us.

"I'll have a latte," Morgan said.

The man shook his head and gestured at the illustrated signs that hung over the counter — the menu. I scanned them.

"I don't think they have latte," I told Morgan.

"Fine," she said. "Cappuccino, then."

The man shook his head again.

"Morgan, I think your choices are coffee, tea, or beer."

She looked at me as if I must surely be mistaken.

"Espresso?" she said to the man.

He shook his head a third time.

"Two coffees," I said.

The man shuffled away.

"Perfect," Morgan said, in a tone that made it clear that it wasn't even on the same planet as perfect.

"Let's drink our coffee, get warm, and go over what we found out. Then we can get out of here," I said. My father had been right. When you start out knowing next to nothing about a person, and when that person doesn't have any of the regular forms of identification and isn't plugged into any of the regular types of networks, like home or family or job or school, it takes a lot of legwork just to gather some puzzle pieces, never mind to assemble the puzzle itself. "I'll go first."

"No, *I'll* go first," Morgan said. "I want to get this stuff out of my head and out of my life."

The sad-looking man slid a couple of cups of murky coffee in front of us. Nestled next to each on the saucer were two little plastic containers of cream. Morgan peered at them as if they contained poison. But she peeled the tops off both of them, sniffed the contents, dumped them into her cup, and stirred. She took a sip and made a face.

"Well, at least it's hot," I said.

"Says who?" she said. She made a face, pushed her coffee aside, and started to tell me what she had found out:

One: "He shopped, if you can call it that, in at least three of the six thrift shops that are within walking distance of the drop-in centre. I say *at least* because the people I talked to at the other three thrift shops couldn't say for sure whether he had ever been in their stores. That photo that Mr. Donovan gave us isn't the greatest." We had made a photocopy of it. Morgan had taken the original with her. I'd shown the copy to a few people, but Mr. Duffy's face was pretty hard to make out. "But for sure Mr. Duffy visited three places on and off over the years, always looking for cheap stuff — you know, a pair of pants, a shirt, a sweater, stuff for winter. But — and explain this to me, will you? — lately he started looking for other stuff: clothes for a small girl and a warm coat for a woman. When he bought that stuff, he always ended up bringing it back a couple of days later. *Always.* What do you think that's all about?"

I had no idea.

Two: "There are two drugstores in the area and two small grocery stores. The people in all of those places recognized Mr. Duffy. They all acted like I was crazy when I asked about him. They said he was a nuisance. One of the drugstores got a clerk to follow him around whenever he was in the store because they were sure he was stealing stuff. But they never actually caught him. The man who owns one of the grocery stores said the same thing — except that he actually caught Mr. Duffy in the act. Guess what he was taking? Packages of spices. The man said coriander, cumin — stuff like that." She looked intently at me, checking, I think, to see if I grasped what she was saying. "Fruit, bread, vegetables, even canned goods — that would make sense. But why would a homeless guy steal spices? The man said Mr. Duffy begged him to let him keep the stuff. The guy finally gave in, but he told Mr. Duffy that he'd call the police if he ever came back. He said Mr. Duffy was so grateful that he actually thanked him."

Three: "I went to the public library. Sometimes people like Mr. Duffy go there to get cool in the summer or to get warm in the winter. The librarian I talked to was really nice. She remembered him and said mostly he was well behaved. She said there are several homeless people who stop by regularly. They just want a place to sit for a while. A lot of them read the daily newspaper and use the bathroom. She said that Mr. Duffy was more interested in magazines. Especially computer magazines. She said it looked like he read them cover to cover. And you know how most libraries usually have a couple of shelves of old books that have been withdrawn from circulation and that they sell for a quarter or fifty cents? She said Mr. Duffy bought one or two almost every time he came in. She said he bought novels, usually classics — Dickens, Tolstoy, Fielding. Lately, though, guess what? He started buying picture books. Kids' books."

Four: "He visited the neighbourhood walk-in

clinic every couple of months." When she saw my expression change, she added, "Yeah, I perked up when I heard that, too. I thought maybe we'd lucked into something. But no one could tell me anything about his medical history, *of course*, because that's confidential. And no one knew anything about him. Apparently he always insisted on seeing the same doctor. Turns out *he's* out of the country right now with *Médecins Sans Frontières* and can't be contacted. I left a voice message on his office phone with your name and phone number in case he ever calls to check his messages. Who knows? Maybe he'll get in touch with you. And that's it — that's all I could get."

I stared at her.

"What?" she said, annoyed — at me, at the spit on her coat, at the lukewarm non-latte coffee, and at our surroundings.

"You did good, Morgan."

"You sound surprised."

I *was* surprised. I had asked Morgan to help me, and she had agreed. But deep down I'd had my doubts about her ability (or willingness) to coax information out of complete strangers about another complete stranger.

"Um . . . " I hesitated to bring this up, considering how well she had done. "I don't suppose you spoke to any of the walk-in clinic clients or any of the thrift store customers, did you?"

"What, and have someone else spit on me? Don't push your luck, Robyn." She leaned back in her chair and crossed her arms over her chest. "So," she said, "what did *you* find out?"

What I had found out:

One: "I talked to intake workers at the two home-less shelters around here. They both said more or less the same thing. They know him only by the name Duffy. They have no idea where he came from. They have no idea what his past life was. They have no idea how he ended up on the street."

"Are you detecting a pattern here, Robyn?" Morgan said.

I continued: "One of the intake workers I talked to has been working at the shelter for maybe five years. He said that Mr. Duffy used to sleep at the shelter from time to time, but not very often. Both of them said that he didn't feel comfortable at the shelters." Ben had told me the same thing.

"But you hear yourself, right, Robyn? Mr. Duffy did know where the shelters were. He could have gone to one of them if he'd wanted to. He didn't *have* to sleep outside."

Maybe.

"They also said that in the past few months, they'd caught him sneaking in a couple of times and stealing stuff. They never pressed charges. They just made him leave. And both of them said that up until recently, Mr. Duffy drank *a lot*. They said most of the money he made panhandling probably went to buying booze."

Morgan reached for her coffee cup, and for a moment I thought the caffeine addict in her was going to win out over the quality-snob. But, no. She sighed and tucked her hands firmly in her lap.

Two: "Mr. Duffy was a regular at the soup kitchen at St. Brigid's Church. They offer a hot meal there at noon every Tuesday and Thursday. He showed up there at least once a week. He never talked to anyone. He never caused any trouble, either — until recently, when he started filling his pockets with extra food, which is strictly against the rules. They let you take a sandwich and a piece of fruit for later in the day, but that's it. Mr. Duffy started taking more."

Three: "I described Mr. Duffy and showed his picture around in ten, maybe eleven, coffee shops and fast-food restaurants in the area where he panhandled." I had canvassed both staff and customers. "I don't think most people pay much attention to what's going on around them. Only two people recognized him, and one of them wasn't one hundred percent sure. They both said he came in from time to time, bought a coffee, and then sat at a table until they had to ask him to leave. Both places have twenty-minute maximums so people can't sit forever over one cup of coffee. Only one person, a guy who works at a place called the Black Cat Café, knew Mr. Duffy's name. *That* person said he let Mr. Duffy use the phone a few times — which he wasn't supposed to do — including a couple of days ago. But he doesn't know who Mr. Duffy called."

Four: "There are dozens of underground parking garages in the area." They were all cold and horrible and scary. But I had trudged down to the toll booth in all of them and showed the picture that Mr. Donovan had given us. "They all said the same thing, Morgan. They always find homeless people — usually more than one — sleeping somewhere inside when the weather is cold. Usually in the stairwells, if they can get in. And usually they let them stay, at least until about seven in the morning when the commuters start to arrive. Apparently, people who drive their cars to work don't want to have to look at homeless people trying to stay warm. But nobody remembered Mr. Duffy specifically."

"Great," Morgan said. "So we froze our butts off all day and, basically, we don't know any more about Mr. Duffy than we did when we started."

"We know a few things," I said.

"Nothing that's going to help Ben. We still don't know his first name. We don't know anything about his past life. We don't know why he's homeless. We don't even know where he's from." She stood up. "Let's get out of here."

I glanced at my watch. "We got down here far too late to catch people on their way into work."

"So?"

"So, people will be heading home soon. Mr. Duffy panhandled in the same location every day. Maybe some people gave money to him regularly. Maybe some of them know something about him."

Morgan shook her head. "No way," she said.

"No way what?"

"You want to stand out in the street accosting people, don't you?"

"Well, I — "

"How are you even going to get them to stop?"

Good question. "Maybe if we — "

"We?" Morgan said. "I knew it. You're my best friend, Robyn. I'd do anything for you — up to a point. But my feet are sore, I have a headache, I have dried spit all over my coat, and I promised Billy I'd meet him at — " She consulted her watch. " — right about now. I gotta run. Come on, Robyn, let's call it a day."

"You go," I said. My feet were sore, too. I also had a headache. I didn't have spit on my coat, but I *was* discouraged. Still — "I'm going to stick around."

Morgan glanced at the three occupied stools, then at the four occupied tables, and finally at me. "I don't think this is the best place for a girl alone — "

"I don't mean here," I said. "I'm going to try to talk to people who might have given Mr. Duffy money. I'll have to do it sooner or later. I might as well get it over with." I dug out some money and slapped it onto the table to pay for our coffees.

We went outside. It was colder now than it had been earlier, or maybe it only seemed that way after we'd been inside for a while.

"Robyn, are you sure?"

I nodded. How hard could it be, right?

Chapter 8

Problem: How do you convince tired, busy people, who are hurrying through a cold, dark evening to their cars or to catch a bus or subway or train so that they can get home to their families or their dogs or their cats, to stop and chat? And, once they've stopped, how do you find out what, if anything, they know about a scruffy, scarred, cantankerous old homeless man who had recently frozen to death?

I stood near the corner outside the medium-sized office building that, according to Andrew, was where Mr. Duffy panhandled on weekdays. It was the same building where I had seen him the first day I went to the drop-in centre. In another thirty minutes, people would start to pour out of the building — and all of the surrounding buildings. Some of them must have paused at least once to throw money into Mr. Duffy's hat, otherwise why would he have come back to the same spot every day? But how would I get any of them to stop to talk to me? If I approached one person, I would miss five or ten other people — maybe people who knew something — while I explained what I was doing to that one person, who might know nothing at all. I thought for a few moments and then headed across the street.

* * *

It took longer than I had anticipated to prepare. By the time I got back to the spot where Mr. Duffy used to panhandle, there were only two thoughts on my mind: 1) I hope this works, and 2) Am I ever glad that Morgan can't see me now.

Then: "Robyn?"

I whirled around. "Ben? What are you doing here?"

What he was doing was staring incredulously at me. When he finished reading the front of the home-made sandwich-board sign that I was wearing, he circled around to read the back. He said, "Do you think that's going to work?"

I shrugged. "It would probably be better if I had someone to help me."

He smiled and, boy, it amazed me how that simple change of expression could transform a person's face.

"What do you want me to do?" he said.

What Ben did was draw attention to me and my signs. A lot of people read them. Some of them shook their heads afterward as if they thought I might be crazy. Some smiled, also as if they thought I might be crazy. A few people came up to me and said that they had heard what had happened, but that they hadn't known that the man who had frozen to death was the same man they passed every day on their way to and from work. A lot of people said that they had dropped money into his hat every now and then, and almost all of them said how sad it was that in such a big, prosperous city, there were so many people who had no roof over their heads. My brilliant plan wasn't exactly an overwhelming success. A grand total of four people told me that they had actually exchanged words with Mr. Duffy.

"I used to buy him tea on the really cold days," one of them, an older woman, said. "I can't remember how I found out that he liked tea, but he did. He preferred it to coffee. I remember the first time I offered him a cup, I was nervous. I thought he might be insulted. But he wasn't. He thanked me so politely. But that's all I know about him."

"I heard about that man who froze to death," said another of them, a man with an expensive-looking briefcase. "That was him, huh?" He shook his head. He really seemed to care. "I wish I knew more about him," he said. "But I don't. Mostly he didn't say much. I remember one time, though, after I'd been on vacation for a month, he mentioned he hadn't seen me around. He asked me if I'd been sick. That really surprised me, because, as I say, he never said much. When I told him I'd been out west, he said he bet the daffodils were out on the coast already. I remember being surprised at that, too, because I hadn't given much thought to where he might have come from or where he might have visited. You don't, do you, when you see someone panhandling? So I asked him if that was where he was from." I held my breath. Maybe I was finally going to learn something about Mr. Duffy. "He didn't answer," the man said.

I tried to hide my disappointment.

"He'd had a head injury," I said. "Maybe he couldn't remember."

The man shook his head. "If it wasn't for bad luck, I guess he'd have no luck at all, huh?" Before he left, he asked me for the name of the drop-in centre. He said he was going to make a donation. He said it was the least he could do.

"I tell you what," the third person, another man, said. "He knew something about computers. I had dropped some money into his hat — every day at the end of the day I drop all my spare change into some panhandler's hat. Why not? I've done well for myself in this business. And who wants to drag around a pocketful of coins? Anyway, a week or so ago, I'd dropped all of my change into his hat and I was talking to a buddy of mine, a software developer, like me. We were just chit-chatting and my buddy mentioned this project he was working on that had him stumped, and the old guy — what did you say his name was? Duffy? — he gave my buddy a suggestion. While he was talking, the lights came on in my buddy's eyes. That old guy knew what he was talking about. Turned out it was a good suggestion. In fact, just the other day my buddy asked me if I'd seen the guy around. He wanted to talk to him. You say he's the guy who froze to death, huh? What a terrible way to go." He dug out his wallet and pressed a wad of twenties into my hand. "You give that to that drop-in centre of yours," he said. "It's not much, but . . . " He shrugged.

And, finally, from a grandmotherly woman who turned out to be a family court judge: "I heard about what happened. What a shame, especially in a big city like this. That little girl is going to miss him."

"Little girl?" I glanced at Ben to see if he had heard and if he knew anything about a little girl. He looked as surprised as I was. "What little girl?"

"There was a little girl who used to come by and talk to him," the woman said. "My office is right across the street." She pointed to an old and elegant stone building across from the glass and steel building where Mr. Duffy used to panhandle. "He used to smile when he saw her coming. I think it's the only time I ever saw him smile."

"Do you know who she is?" I said.

The woman shook her head. "Just a little girl. She looks about five or six years old. She always comes by with her mother. At least, I assume it's her mother. They're South Asian. Indian or Sri Lankan, I'm not sure."

"Do you know if they came regularly, maybe at a particular time or on a particular day?"

The woman shook her head again. "I didn't pay that much attention. I just used to look out the window sometimes and see the little girl and her mother, and the little girl would be talking to the man you're asking about."

"Do you know when they were here last?"

"I'm sorry," she said. "I really don't know anything else."

As she walked away, an elegantly dressed man came up to me and said he'd been listening to what I had been saying and that he thought what I was doing was "admirable."

"It's always so gratifying to see a young person take such an active interest in the community," he said.

"Did you know the man who used to. panhandle here?" I said.

"To be honest," he said. "I'm not sure. I've been tossing coins into several hats every day. It will probably sound terrible to you, considering what you're trying to do here, but I don't pay a lot of attention. I see the hat or whatever container they're using to collect money, and I throw something in."

I remembered the first time I had seen Mr. Duffy. He had a face that was impossible to forget. But when I described him, the man shrugged apologetically. Maybe Mr. Duffy hadn't looked up.

"I'm in town for the next couple of weeks. My company is setting up a new office right up there," the man said, pointing. "If it will help, I'll ask around the building and see if anyone there talked to the man and knows anything."

"I'd appreciate it." I hunted around for a piece of paper, scribbled down my name and cell phone number, and handed it to him. "This is where you can reach me," I said.

"Robyn," he said, reading what I had written. "I'll

remember that. Tell me, how did you come to know this man?"

"I didn't really know him," I admitted. "But my friend Ben did." I waved Ben over and introduced him. "Ben volunteers at the drop-in centre that Mr. Duffy liked to go to."

The man chatted with Ben for a few moments about the drop-in centre and the work it did. Then he pulled out a business card and wrote something on the back.

"Here's a number where you can reach me," he said. "I'd be interested in knowing if you ever solve this little mystery of yours."

I tucked the card in my pocket.

"Nice guy," Ben said.

"All the people who stopped to talk were nice," I said. And the four who had taken a few moments to try to talk to Mr. Duffy made me feel ashamed of myself. The most I had ever done was drop a loonie or a toonie into a hat.

The rush-hour crowd had thinned, and I was shivering uncontrollably as I pulled off my sandwich-board sign.

"I guess that expensive jacket isn't as warm as it looks, huh?" Ben said.

"For your information, I've been out all day talking to people — "

"I'm just teasing," he said. His voice was gentle. For once he didn't seem to be angry with me or to be making fun of me. "Come on," he said. "Let's go someplace where you can warm up."

He steered me to a small, cosy, delightfully warm restaurant. We claimed a booth near the back and shucked our coats and hats. Ben dropped his back-pack onto the floor beside him. After a waiter handed us menus, I glanced at Ben.

"What are you doing down here anyway?" I said. "Are you checking up on me?"

"Actually, yes," Ben said.

That made me angry. "I told you I'd do whatever I could to find out about Mr. Duffy. Didn't you believe me?"

"Of course I did," he said.

"But you still came to check up on me?"

"I came to make sure you were all right. And to see if I could help."

Wait a minute. "How did you even know I was here?"

He smiled at me. "Billy's girlfriend called me."

"Morgan?"

He nodded. "She told me what you were doing. She *suggested* that I come down here." He laughed. "Actually, it was more than a suggestion. She said she thought it was totally unfair that you were, as she put it, freezing your butt off down here while I was lounging around in a nice, warm house."

That sounded like Morgan — both what she had said and what she had done. I bet I knew why she'd done it, too, and it wasn't just because she thought that Ben should be helping me. She'd dropped enough hints. She thought Ben would be the perfect replacement for Nick. But I wasn't interested in a replacement.

"She's right," Ben said. "I shouldn't leave it all to you. I've been thinking about what I said to you. I was mad. I hate that Mr. Duffy died the way he did. I hate that he's just some anonymous homeless person that nobody cares about and that his family, if he has one, probably has no idea that he's even dead. But I shouldn't have taken out my frustration on you."

We ordered. While we waited for our food, I said, "Well, at least we know a little more about him now than we did before."

"We do?"

"Sure we do. You heard what some of those people out there said. I'd be willing to bet that Mr. Duffy spent at least some time out west. We know that he liked tea. We know that he knew enough about computers, either from reading computer magazines at the public library or from something in his past, to impress someone who's in the computer business."

"He liked to surf the Internet at the drop-in centre sometimes," Ben said. "I asked him one time what kind of sites he liked to visit, but he didn't answer."

"Well, he may not have talked much, but he wasn't completely anti-social, either. And that little girl made him smile." I thought about that for a moment. "The librarian Morgan talked to said he bought used paperback novels from the library."

"I know," Ben said.

"You do?"

"The two books he had with him? They were from the library. They were stamped *Withdrawn*."

"Morgan said that up until recently he bought adult books," I told Ben. "Then about six months ago, he started buying children's books. Maybe they were for that little girl. He also bought children's clothes at a second-hand clothing store. But he always brought them back for a refund." I hadn't figured that one out. "How long did you know Mr. Duffy, Ben?"

"Almost a year. I started volunteering at the drop-in centre last January. It was my New Year's resolution — do something good for someone else."

"What was he like when you first met him?"

"What do you mean?"

"Morgan and I talked to a lot of people today. From what everyone said, it seems that something changed in Mr. Duffy's life about six months ago." I went over everything that Morgan and I had found out. "Up until six months ago he was drinking. Then he stopped. Up until six months ago, he didn't cause trouble at any of the shelters or soup kitchens he visited. Then he started taking things — food, mostly. Up until recently, he visited second-hand stores and thrift stores to buy clothes for himself. Then, all of a sudden, he started buying children's clothes."

"Which he returned," Ben said.

I nodded. "Up until about six months ago, no one at any of the stores he went in ever complained about him. Then he started stealing. He stole spices from a grocery store." I asked Ben the same question Morgan had asked me. "Why would a homeless man with no access to a kitchen steal spices? You can't do anything with them unless you're cooking."

"Maybe he gave them to Betty," Ben said.

"We talked to Betty. She would have mentioned it." It was so frustrating to have uncovered such tantalizing little bits and pieces but to be no closer to the truth. "I have no idea what it all adds up to," I said. "It's almost as if he didn't want anyone to know anything about him."

The waiter returned with our food. I couldn't believe how hungry I was. I tucked into my grilled chicken salad with enthusiasm.

"Do you think maybe we should just leave it alone?" Ben said. "Drop the idea of a memorial service? You know, respect his privacy?"

"I don't know. Maybe." What to do about the memorial service was Ben's decision. I was thinking about the little girl and her mother and what that woman had said about them. And about the spices Mr. Duffy had stolen. I wondered if the woman and the little girl knew that Mr. Duffy had died. "What happened to the books Mr. Duffy had with him?"

"I have them right here," Ben said. He picked his backpack up off the floor. I stared at it.

"What's that?" I said.

"What's what?"

"That." I pointed to the crest on his backpack. I hadn't noticed it before. "Does that say Ashdale Academy?"

Ben's cheeks turned pink.

"It does, doesn't it? How come you have a backpack with an Ashdale crest on it? Do you go to Ashdale?"

He looked at the few remaining French fries on his plate.

"Do you, Ben?" Ashdale Academy was a private boys' school uptown. I'd heard it referred to as the most expensive, most exclusive boys' school in the city.

He straightened up slowly, as if it were an ordeal, and nodded.

"Uh-huh," I said, digesting this new fact. "So where exactly did you get off giving me a hard time because of how *I* dress and the car *my* dad drives, when you go to the most exclusive school in town?"

"Would it help if I apologized?"

"It would help if you explained."

He drew in a deep breath. "Okay," he said. "The first time I saw you, I thought I knew you. I mean, I thought I knew your type. I thought you were like the girls who live in my neighbourhood. The girls who go to St. Mildred's." St. Mildred's was the most exclusive private *girls'* school in the city. "Most of them have no idea what real life is like. Their idea of privation is having to wait a week until the Prada bag they ordered comes in."

"You think I'm like *that?*"

"Thought," he said. "Definitely past tense. I was wrong. I'm sorry." He looked at me, and, just for a moment, I felt drawn to him. Then I thought about Nick.

"Right," I said. "Let's see those books." I held out my hand.

"I don't think they're going to tell us anything.

They're just beat up second-hand books." Ben fished them out of his Ashdale-crested backpack.

Ours hands touched as Ben passed the books to me, and our eyes met again. I looked away quickly and told myself that I didn't want to get involved with anyone else, even if he turned out to be a whole lot nicer and a whole lot more caring than I had originally thought. I told myself that Nick was the one for me — Nick, who had left town without a word to anyone. A wave of anger washed over me, I blocked both Ben and Nick out of my mind, and turned my attention to the two books.

Chapter 9

Both of the battered paperbacks that had been in Mr. Duffy's pockets when he died were written by Charles Dickens. One was *Great Expectations*. The other, *Hard Times*. I flipped through them. A business card was tucked in the pages of the first book. I looked at it. It was a card from one of the best hotels in the city. I held it up so that Ben could see it.

"He must have picked it up somewhere," Ben said. "He was probably using it as a bookmark."

I held the front and back covers of each book and shook them gently. A slip of paper fell out of one of them. I picked it up and looked at it.

"Is it anything useful?" Ben said.

"It's a cash register receipt." I studied the faint ink. "From a thrift shop." In fact, it was from one of the shops that Morgan had visited only this morning. "But I can't tell what he bought — it only says *clothing* and the price. And the date. About two months ago."

"In other words, not useful," Ben said.

I turned the receipt over. Someone had written what appeared to be a phone number on the other side, followed by the letter F.

"Would you recognize Mr. Duffy's handwriting if you saw it?" I said.

Ben shook his head. I looked at the phone number again. It had been written in pencil and had faded or been worn out, but it was still legible. The numbers were beautifully formed in a thin, elegant hand.

"It doesn't look like a man's handwriting," I said. "And it sure doesn't look like the handwriting you'd expect from a homeless person."

"A homeless person who likes tea and Charles Dickens and talks about daffodils blooming out west?" Ben said.

He had a point. Before today, I had thought of Mr. Duffy as just a shabby, crazy old man who stole cookies from the kitchen at the drop-in centre and shoved people when he got angry, a man who was only what you saw and whose past I had never considered. But he had come from somewhere. And he must have started out like everyone else: young and with the potential to become almost anything. It was possible that he had spent his whole life on the street — anything is possible — but it didn't seem likely. There had to be a way to find out more about him. There just had to be. I looked down at the faded receipt from the thrift shop. Then I dug into my bag, pulled out my cell phone, and started to punch in numbers.

"Who are you calling?" Ben said.

A phone rang somewhere at the other end of the line. It rang again and again until finally someone said, "Hello?" It was a man's voice.

"Hello," I said. "Who am I talking to?"

"Who do you *want* to talk to?" the man said. He sounded annoyed.

"Is Morgan there?"

Ben gave me a funny look. "Morgan is at Billy's house," he said.

Instead of telling me that I had the wrong number, the man at the other end of the line called out, "Is there a Morgan here?" That told me that the number on the back of the sales receipt didn't belong to a private residence. I must have called some kind of public place. The man came back on the line. "You're out of luck," he said. "There's no one here named Morgan."

"Um, where is here, exactly?" I said.

"Look, sweetheart, you made the call. I just picked up the phone. Your friend isn't here, and a dryer has just opened up. If I don't grab it, someone else will and I'll have to go home with wet undies, you know what I'm saying?"

Dryer? Wet undies? It must be a coin laundry.

"Morgan left me a message," I said. "She wanted me to bring her some fabric softener, but she didn't give me the name of the place or the address."

I heard the man shout, "Touch that dryer and you die!"

"Hello? Hello?"

He told me the name of the coin laundry and the main intersection. Then he hung up.

"What was that all about?" Ben said.

"The phone number on the back of this receipt — I think it's a pay phone at a laundromat a couple of blocks from the drop-in centre."

Ben sighed. "In other words, the place where Mr. Duffy washed his clothes."

"I guess." I started to hand him back the books, but Ben shook his head.

"Every time I look at those books, I feel terrible. I know Mr. Duffy didn't have much — but to think that a couple of second-hand books were his only possessions . . . I hate to throw them out, but . . . "

"If you want, I'll hang onto them for you. If you want them back, just let me know."

Ben nodded gratefully, and I stuffed the books into my bag.

"Come on," Ben said. "I'll walk you to the bus."

I fished out my wallet, but Ben waved it away.

"Dinner's on me," he said. "After everything you've done, I feel I owe you one." On the way out of the restaurant, he said, "By the way, the funeral is the day after tomorrow."

"The day after tomorrow? But we don't know — "

"It is when it is. The way things are going, we won't be able to say much about him, and it looks like there will never be a complete name to put on the headstone."

"Headstone?" I knew the city would pay for the funeral and the burial. But a headstone? "Aren't those expensive?"

"I'm going to pay for it — well, with a lot of help

from my father." There was no warmth in his words. "At first he said no. He said it was a waste of money." He looked fiercely at me. "He was going to buy me a car for Christmas. I told him I wanted this instead. Maybe no one can say much about Mr. Duffy at his funeral, but if we ever find out his real name, he's going to have a headstone."

"I wish I could have done more," I said.

He shook his head. "I gave you an impossible mission, Robyn. But you did great. Really."

* * *

I almost fell over when my mother gave me permission to go to the funeral. I had braced myself for an argument.

"My heart isn't made of stone," she said when she saw how surprised I was. "That man's death is a tragedy. And, anyway, I doubt there's going to be much serious work done at school this morning."

There were a lot more people in the church than I had expected. Mr. Donovan was right up front with Ben. So were Betty and a few other volunteers. I recognized some of the drop-in centre clients, too. And in the middle of the church but twisted around in her seat and watching the door — looking for me, it turned out — was Morgan, sitting next to Billy. She waved when she saw me. I gestured to her from the back of the church. She said something to Billy, who turned and smiled at me. Then she scooted out of the pew and came to meet me.

"We saved you a place," she said.

"I want to sit in the back."

"But Ben's up front. Don't you — "

"If I sit in the back, I'll be able to see everyone who comes in," I said.

"Are you expecting someone?"

"I'm not sure. Maybe."

"I'll go and get Billy," she said.

I shook my head. "You guys might as well stay put. I'll catch up with you afterward."

Morgan returned to her place next to Billy. I checked out the pews at the rear of the church. The last one on the right was empty, and there was only one person sitting in the one on the left — Andrew. He started to smile when he saw me and then quickly hid his mouth with his hand.

"What are you doing way back here?" I said, sliding into the pew beside him.

He shrugged shyly. "I like to be near the exit. You know, just in case."

Just in case of what? I wondered.

"What about you?" he said. "Don't you want to sit up there with your friends?"

"I want to see who comes and goes."

"You mean, you're staking out the place?"

"Sort of. I'm kind of hoping that a woman who knew Mr. Duffy will show up."

Just as the service started, someone slipped into the same pew as Andrew and I. I turned to see if it was a woman, but it wasn't. It was a man in a long overcoat. He had a black tuque pulled down over his eyebrows, which he did not remove. He looked at Andrew and me before turning his attention to the front of the church. From the look of him, I guessed he was a client of the drop-in centre. I wondered how well he had known Mr. Duffy and if Mr. Duffy had ever spoken to him.

I continued to scan the crowd during the first half of the service. At one point, Mr. Donovan got up and said a few words about Mr. Duffy. Mostly he said how quiet Mr. Duffy had been and how he had never talked much about himself. Then Ben stood up and faced everyone. He had a sheet of paper in his hand and he glanced at it before he started speaking.

"I didn't know Mr. Duffy well," he said. "Nobody did. Like Mr. Donovan said, he kept mostly to himself. And that was his right." He looked out at the people scattered among the pews. Then he looked down at the piece of paper again. After a moment, he crumpled it, drew in a deep breath, and said, "It was his right to keep to himself. It was his right not to talk about himself, about who he was or where he came from. But I can't help thinking that it's too bad we don't know more about Mr. Duffy, because if we did, maybe people would care more about what happened to him and what could just as easily happen to other people like him. There are a lot of people like Mr. Duffy out there, and most of the time, people don't think about them. They're real people and they matter as much as anyone else, but they're homeless. If people hear that a homeless man died, that makes one kind of picture in their minds. But if they hear that a man who loved flowers and little children died, a man who liked to drink tea and read novels by

Charles Dickens, a man who maybe had a family somewhere but who had fallen on hard times, that makes a whole different picture. Mr. Duffy froze to death in the middle of a big, wealthy city in a big, wealthy country. He froze to death because he didn't have a home to call his own. But because nobody knows anything about him, they don't get angry about it. And if we don't get angry — good and angry — about the fact that some of our neighbours don't have a roof over their heads, then how are things ever going to change? How are we going to make sure that something like this never happens again?"

He stopped abruptly and looked at Mr. Donovan. "I'm sorry," he said. "But that's how I feel."

There was dead silence in the church. Then Andrew started to clap, quietly and slowly. Someone in front of us joined in. Then someone else and someone else, until finally everyone was clapping. Ben was still standing at the front of the church. His face turned red. He said something to the minister and then went back to his seat. The minister waited until everyone had quieted down. Then he said, "I don't believe I have ever heard applause at a funeral service, but I must say, I think that the sentiment expressed by the previous speaker deserves the endorsement that it received. In Luke, Chapter Three, Verse Eleven, John the Baptist says, 'Let the man who has two coats give one to the man who has none.' I think what our young friend was expressing just now is exactly that . . . "

I didn't pay attention to the rest of what the minister said because I was watching a woman walk up one side of the church. She was wearing a thin coat and had a scarf over her head. Under the coat, she had on brown and gold pyjama-like pants and a matching tunic. She was carrying a small, plastic-wrapped bunch of flowers and was holding a little girl by the hand. The woman hesitated when she reached the front of the church. She looked at the people in the pews. Then she pulled herself straight, as if she had just made a decision, and led the little girl to Mr. Duffy's casket. She laid the bunch of flowers on top of it. Then, head bowed, she led the little girl back the way they had come.

"Andrew, do me a favour?" I whispered as I watched the woman and the little girl head for the door. "If I'm not back before the service ends, tell Morgan — my friend up there — that I'll call her. Okay?"

Andrew nodded. He didn't ask where I was going.

I got up and hurried out of the church. By the time I got outside, the woman and the little girl were scurrying down the street. I ran after them. Maybe they weren't the two people the judge had seen with Mr. Duffy, but they sure fit the description. And if they were, they might know something.

Both the woman and the little girl looked impossibly underdressed for the cold. Both of them were wearing cheap sneakers instead of warm boots. Both had on thin, stretchy gloves, the kind you can buy at a dollar store and that do next to nothing to keep your hands warm. Both had scarves wound around their heads instead of hats, and both wore thin coats that might have protected them from rain, but were all but useless in keeping out the frigid December air. I caught up with them while they were waiting for a red light to turn green.

"Excuse me," I said.

The woman's dark eyes looked enormous in her thin face. She gathered the little girl against her and stared at me. She was shivering.

"I'm sorry to bother you," I said, "but I saw you at the church."

She just stared at me.

"I wanted to talk to you about Mr. Duffy."

"Duffy?" she said.

"You were just at the church," I said. "At his funeral."

The little girl looked up at her mother and said something in a small voice, something that I couldn't understand. The woman scooped her up and held her tightly.

"Someone told me that they'd seen you and your daughter talking to Mr. Duffy on the street," I said. I smiled at the little girl, who responded by burrowing her face in her mother's scarf.

"Someone talked to you about me?" the woman said, her eyes widening in alarm. "Someone was watching me?" My father would have placed her accent immediately. He had a good ear and loved to surprise people by pinpointing their country or region of origin based on a few words or sentences. But I was hopeless at it.

"No, no," I said. "No one was watching you. It's

just that I've been trying to find people who knew Mr. Duffy, and someone said that they'd seen a woman and a little girl talking to him. So I was wondering — "

The woman's eyes shifted from me to somewhere over my shoulder.

"I'm sorry," she said. She looked nervous all of a sudden. "I must go."

Behind me, a voice said something in a language I didn't understand. I turned around and saw an angry-looking man who was as underdressed for the cold as the woman and the little girl. Like them, he was wearing shoes instead of boots and had only a light jacket over top of what looked like work clothes. The jacket had a company name and logo sewn onto it. He scowled at me as he took the little girl from the woman's arms. He said something else to the woman. She shook her head as she answered. As he started to walk away, carrying the little girl, the woman looked apologetically at me. Then she hurried after him.

"Wait," I called. "If I could just ask you a few questions . . . "

The man turned and glared at me. He quickened his pace. I didn't know what to do. For some reason, the woman seemed nervous, and it was clear that this person, who I could only assume was her husband, didn't want her talking to me. But why not?

I watched them disappear around a corner. Then, as if I'd been tethered to them and had no choice, I started to follow them. By the time I got to the corner, they were at the top of the next street. They turned again. I picked up my pace. But when I reached the corner where they had made their second turn, they had vanished. I stared up the street. There were at least thirty or forty houses on each side. They could have gone into any one of them. I stood there for a moment, watching for movement. Nothing.

Discouraged, I headed back to the church. On the way, I noticed something I hadn't seen when I was following the family — I had passed a laundromat. It was the same one I had called after finding the phone number that had been tucked inside one of Mr. Duffy's books.

Chapter 10

My cell phone trilled — again.

"Yes?" I said wearily.

It was Morgan. "Explain to me one more time why I'm freezing my butt off out here in the cold *again* instead of finishing my Christmas shopping at a nice, warm mall," she said. "In fact, explain to me why every time I volunteer to help you — or Billy — I always end up numb with cold."

Morgan had not been my first choice as a helper. I had approached Billy, thinking that he would agree right away — and he would have if he weren't already scheduled to be at the Humane Society. Nor had Morgan actually volunteered. On the contrary, she had wanted to go home and soak in a nice hot bubble bath because, as she put it, "That church was hot and some of those people smelled bad to begin with and it only got worse when they got overheated — no offence to anyone." Then she had wanted to indulge in her favourite pastime — shopping.

Instead, I had talked her into coming back downtown with me.

I sighed. "Are you going to call me every two minutes to complain?" I said, glad that we were communicating by cell phone and not face to face.

"We've been out here for nearly an hour, Robyn. The sun is going down. It's getting *really* cold."

"If he's going to show, he's going to show soon," I said.

"How do you know he's going to show at all?"

Boy, *that* question again.

"Because he was wearing a Night Owl Cleaners jacket," I said, *again*. "Night Owl cleans office buildings." I knew that because I had been at my mother's office many times after hours when the Night Owl cleaners were there. According to my mother, it was a huge company that had practically cornered the market on the downtown office towers. "They start as soon as everyone else has gone home, which is usually around five-thirty or six o'clock. So if he works for Night Owl, he's going to have to leave home soon or he'll be late for work."

"*If* he actually works for Night Owl," Morgan said grumpily.

"He was wearing a Night Owl jacket."

"Jason Ransome wears army fatigues to school — what a loser! — but he's not a soldier," Morgan said. "He gets them at a second-hand store. He thinks they make him look cool."

I checked my watch. "If we don't see him by six o'clock, we'll leave," I said. "I'll even buy you a latte."

"And a biscotti," Morgan said. "Chocolate."

"Done," I said. If there was one thing I had learned during my long friendship with Morgan, it was that bribery definitely worked.

I had figured it this way: I knew which street the woman and the little girl lived on, but I didn't know which house. So I had enlisted Morgan to stand at one end of the street while I stood at the other, watching to see which house the man came out of. My plan was that after he was gone, we could go and talk to the woman. Maybe she wouldn't be so nervous this time. I wasn't one hundred percent positive, but I had the feeling that she might know Mr. Duffy better than anyone else I had encountered so far. Mr. Duffy had bought children's clothes at the second-hand store. He had bought children's books at the library. He had stolen spices from a grocery store. I could be wrong, but I thought probably he had done those things for that woman and her little girl.

My cell phone trilled yet again.

"I'll buy you a *box* of biscotti, Morgan," I said, "if you'll just hang in a little longer — "

"He's a scrawny guy, right?" Morgan said. Her voice was muffled and hard to make out. "Dark hair, thin face, wearing a short jacket?"

"Morgan, I can hardly hear you."

Nothing. Silence.

"Morgan?" I peered up the street but didn't see her. "Morgan? Are you still there?"

"He just went past me and got on a bus," Morgan

said, her voice loud and clear now. "This Night Owl Cleaners . . . Do their jackets have a big yellow circle on them with what looks like an owl in the centre of it?"

"You have to ask?" I said.

"Then that must have been him."

"Did you see which house he came out of?"

"I sure did. And I heard what you said about a box of biscotti. I'm going to hold you to that."

I signed off and hurried up the street to meet her. I had a bag in one hand.

"That's the place," Morgan said, pointing to a run-down, two-storey brick house.

We climbed the rickety wooden steps and knocked on the door. No one answered. A man carrying two green garbage bags appeared from around the side of the house. He glanced at us as he toted the bags to the curb. Then he disappeared around the side of the house again. He was back a minute later with a couple more bags. He paused and looked at us again.

"What's his problem?" Morgan said.

I knocked again, louder this time. Still no answer.

"The woman and the little girl must have gone out before I saw the man leave," Morgan said.

"Maybe," I said. Now I wished that I hadn't stopped off at that store on our way. I wished we'd started watching the street sooner.

"You girls looking for someone?" the man called to us from the curb.

"Someone needs a hobby," Morgan muttered.

"Maybe he knows her." I turned to the man.

"We're looking for the woman who lives here."

He gave me a strange look. "There's six women who live here," he said. "Some guys, too. It's apartments. Knocking on that door — " He nodded at the front door "— won't do you any good." When we didn't move, he shook his head, as if he thought we were slow-witted. "You have to go inside," he said, "and knock on the door of the person you're looking for."

Oh.

Morgan opened the outer door and we stepped into a cramped foyer. I counted six locked mailboxes set into the wall beside the door.

"This place doesn't look big enough for six apartments," Morgan said.

"They must be awfully small," I agreed.

"Imagine bringing up a kid in a place like this," Morgan said. She looked around the bleak foyer. "So, which one are we looking for?"

I looked at the mailboxes. Each one had a name printed on a little card taped to the top of the box. I pulled my wallet out of my bag and fished out the thrift store receipt that Ben and I had found in one of Mr. Duffy's books. One of the name cards on the mailboxes had been printed in what looked like the same slender, elegant handwriting as the telephone number on the back of the receipt. I pointed to it.

"That one," I said. Mailbox number five. "Khan, R."

Morgan looked at the three doors that led off the tiny foyer. "Door number one, door number two, or door number three?" she said.

There was only one way to find out. I opened the

first door. It led to another small foyer in the basement with a door on either side. I crept down just far enough to see the numbers on them — one and two. I retreated to the main foyer and opened the second door, which revealed two more doors and two more numbers — three and four.

"Door number three," I said to Morgan.

She rolled her eyes. "Brilliant powers of deduction, Robyn."

Door number three opened onto a flight of stairs that led to the second floor of the house. At the top were two more doors — apartments five and six. I knocked on the door to number five. At first, I saw light behind the peephole in the door. Then the peephole went dark, a sure sign that someone's eye was pressed up against it. When it finally went light again, I thought the door would open. But it didn't. I knocked again.

"No one's home," Morgan said. To my surprise, she actually sounded disappointed.

I knocked, harder this time. The flimsy door rattled in its frame.

"Robyn, geeze, take a hint," Morgan said. "We'll have to come back another time."

The door opened a few centimetres, startling Morgan, and a woman peeked out over the security chain.

"Hi," I said. "Remember me? I saw you at the funeral. I know you were a friend of Mr. Duffy's. I knew him, too."

The woman looked at us. She shook her head and

started to close the door. I pushed against it to keep it open.

"Please," I said. "I just want to talk to you for a few minutes."

"I must close the door before I can open it," the woman said.

I let go. The door closed, and I heard the rattle of the security chain. A moment later, the door opened again.

The woman inside was small and slender. She had a blanket wrapped around her shoulders for warmth. A small, dark-eyed girl peeked out from behind her.

"You may come in," the woman said.

Morgan and I both wiped our feet on the small mat outside the door before entering.

"How did you know where to find me?" the woman said.

Embarrassed, I explained that I had followed her. "But only because it's important," I said. I explained to her how I knew Mr. Duffy and that I was trying to find out more about him. "I feel partly responsible for what happened," I said.

The woman frowned. "You?" she said. "How are you responsible?"

I told her what had happened at the drop-in centre, how Mr. Duffy had been barred from the centre just before one of the coldest nights of the year and how, because of that, he had frozen to death. The woman listened in silence. When I had finished, she said, "He was difficult to understand. How he acted, I mean. At first, he scared me. But he never scared Yasmin. This is Yasmin." She laid a hand on the head of the little girl who clung to her. "I am Aisha. It is a cold night. Please, let me make you some tea."

We removed our boots and shucked our coats and were both glad — at least, I was, and I imagine that Morgan was — that we were wearing warm sweaters. The two small rooms that made up the tiny apartment were chilly. As I looked around the sparsely furnished place and remembered how underdressed for the weather she, her husband, and their little girl had been, I realized that buying flowers to take to the funeral had been a huge sacrifice of family resources.

"Please, sit," Aisha said, indicating a battered couch against one wall. She disappeared into the small room off the main room — it turned out to be the bathroom — to fill a kettle. She set the kettle on the small, battered stove and turned on a burner. While we waited for the water to boil, we found out a little more about Aisha and her husband Rashid.

They had recently emigrated from Pakistan, thinking that the move would offer more opportunities to Yasmin and to any other children that they might have. They had been told before they left their home that they would have no trouble finding employment and had saved their money so that they would have enough to live on while they got settled and found jobs. Rashid had been a civil engineer in Pakistan. Aisha had been a medical doctor. But neither had been able to find work in their field because their qualifications weren't recognized here. No one would hire Rashid because he didn't have any experience in this country. Before she could practise medicine again, Aisha would have to take exams to qualify her here. They couldn't afford that right now. As it was, she said, they had been in the country for nearly nine months now and had used up almost all of their savings. It had taken Rashid a long time — nearly six months — to find a job. He had worked in telemarketing for a few weeks, but hated it so much that Aisha had insisted he quit.

"Now he cleans office buildings at night," she said. "He does not like it. He feels it demeans him. But what can we do?"

Everything had turned out to be much more expensive than they had expected. And they, like everyone else, had been surprised at how early winter had come this year and at how cold it had been so far. Once again, I remembered how little protection their clothes offered against the cold.

"There are stores where you can buy warm winter clothing second-hand," I said. "But they're clean and in good condition."

"Yes," she said. "I know. I have been to one. I bought a coat for Yasmin. But when Rashid found out that the store was operated by a charity, he made me take it back. He is very proud. He will not accept charity."

I thought about the clothing that Mr. Duffy had bought and then returned. It was starting to make sense.

The kettle started to whistle and Aisha hurried to

the stove to make the tea. She poured it into delicate glass teacups that she had set out on a tray. The tea was milky and smelled sweet and fragrant.

I set my bag on the table and pulled out a box.

"We brought some cupcakes," I said. I had been thinking of the little girl when I bought them. "Chocolate," I said, smiling at Yasmin. "Do you like chocolate?"

Yasmin nodded solemnly and watched me open the box. Her eyes grew big as she approached to look at the sweets inside. She turned to her mother. Aisha said something to her softly. She took three small plates from the cupboard over the stove. She put one of the cupcakes on a plate and handed it to Yasmin. The little girl sat on a chair and delicately attacked it, first peeling off the paper, then breaking off the bottom of the cupcake and eating it in small bites between sips of extra-milky tea, and finally nibbling on the top half of the cupcake, which was covered with thick chocolate frosting.

Aisha insisted that Morgan and I each have a cupcake, but she didn't have one herself.

"About Mr. Duffy," I said at last.

"He was kind to us," Aisha said. "He tried to help us."

"Tried?" Morgan said.

"We met him in the park during the summer. That is to say, Yasmin met him." She looked fondly at her daughter. "She was playing, and she ran across the park while I wasn't looking. All of a sudden, a big dog ran toward her and frightened her."

I looked sympathetically at Yasmin. The same thing had happened to me when I was small, except that the big dog I had encountered in a park had bitten me, giving me a severe case of canine-phobia.

"Then a man — it was Mr. Duffy — came and took the dog by the collar and returned it to its owner, who had not been paying attention to the dog. The man who owned the dog was very rude to Mr. Duffy. He said that his dog was harmless and that it had as much right to be in the park as anyone else. Mr. Duffy tried to tell him that the dog had frightened Yasmin, but the man wouldn't listen. He called Mr. Duffy names. He was rude to him because of the way he looked and the way he dressed. That made me very angry." Her eyes flashed. "When I told the man he should be more polite and he should take care of his dog, he became angry with me, too, and he called me names."

"I'm sorry," I said.

Aisha took a sip of her tea. "I thanked Mr. Duffy for helping Yasmin. He was very quiet. He kept his head down. He wouldn't look at me. I'm not sure, but I think the man with the dog made him feel ashamed of his appearance. His face — " She glanced at Yasmin. "If you didn't know him, he could look very fierce. I think he didn't want to frighten Yasmin the way the dog did. He walked away. A few days later, we saw him in the park again. It was still warm and I had brought our lunch with us so that Yasmin and I could have a picnic. It's much nicer in the park than it is in this flat." She looked around ruefully. "When

I saw him, I wanted to thank him for helping Yasmin, so I invited him to share our lunch. At first he didn't want to. But when Yasmin offered him some food, he finally accepted. He ate with real pleasure." She smiled proudly. "The next day, we saw him again. He had a tin of preserved peaches with him. He wanted me to take it home, but I couldn't. Rashid would want to know where I had got it. If I told him that it was a gift from a stranger, he wouldn't let me keep it. Nor could I tell him that I had bought the peaches. He would want to know why I'd thrown away money on something like that. So Mr. Duffy took the tin to a restaurant across the street from the park and when he came back, it was open and he had plastic spoons and we ate the peaches in the park — the whole tin! They were delicious." She smiled at the memory.

"After that, we often saw him in the park or on the street. He was a poor man," she said. "He would sit on the street and people would give him money. I felt so sorry for him. But he always had something for us. For Yasmin. He liked to bring her cookies." I remembered the ones he had tried to steal from the drop-in centre.

"And spices," I said. "He gave you spices."

"How did you know?" Aisha said.

I told a little white lie. I said that a clerk in a grocery store had told me Mr. Duffy had bought spices.

Aisha nodded. "He also bought warm clothing for us from one of those charity shops. But I had to make him take it back. Rashid would never accept it. Mr.

Duffy didn't understand that. He kept bringing me things for Yasmin, and always I had to ask him to return them so that he could get his money back. He had so little. One time when we were out with Rashid, we saw him and Yasmin ran to talk to him. Rashid didn't like that. He was like the man in the park — he only saw what Mr. Duffy looked like, and he didn't want Yasmin to talk to him. I argued with him later, but it didn't do any good. Rashid can be very stubborn."

I took out the thrift-store receipt with the phone number written on the back of it and the letter F next to it.

"Did you give him this number?" I said.

She nodded. "I know the woman who runs the laundromat. I do my laundry there every Friday morning."

"Is that what the F means?" I said.

"I told him he could reach me there on Fridays. He could leave a message for me there, too, in case anything happened and he needed something. I worried about him, especially in the cold weather. But he never telephoned. He never asked for help."

"Did Mr. Duffy ever talk about his personal life?" I said.

Aisha hesitated for a moment and then shook her head.

"Did you hear the young man who spoke at the funeral?" I said. She nodded. "He liked Mr. Duffy. And he thinks it's terrible that nobody knows anything about him. He thinks that unless he can tell Mr.

Duffy's story — you know, let people know who he was before he ended up on the street, let them understand *how* he ended up on the street — that people will just go on thinking that homeless people aren't people like the rest of us, that they're different, that they deserve to be on the street because they're lazy or stupid or crazy."

"Mr. Duffy was not stupid," Aisha said. She sounded surprised that anyone would think such a thing. "He was very smart. I think he was a professional man before his life changed."

"What makes you think that?"

"He knew a lot. And he read a lot. He liked to go to the library."

"Did he ever talk about what kind of work he used to do?"

She shook her head.

"Did he ever tell you what happened to him, how he ended up on the street?"

She shook her head again.

"Sometimes he had terrible headaches," she said. "He'd had a bad injury. I asked him what had happened to him, but he never told me. Sometimes his eyes looked empty. Sometimes he didn't remember things."

Yasmin scampered back into the room. I hadn't even noticed that she had been gone. She tugged on her mother's tunic and said something softly that I couldn't understand. Then she pressed something into her mother's hand. Aisha sat silently for a moment, clutching whatever Yasmin had just given her, her eyes staring down at the threadbare carpet on the floor.

"I don't know where he came from," she said at last, looking up to meet my eyes. "But one day he said to me, 'Aisha, would *you* take me back?'"

"Back where?" Morgan said.

Aisha shrugged. "I asked him what he meant. But he just shook his head and said he was being foolish. He said probably he had imagined it, probably he was seeing things."

"Seeing what?" I said.

"I don't know. We were talking to him on the street, where he was asking for money, and he asked me. Then he got up and walked away. He didn't even say goodbye to Yasmin. I don't think he was feeling well that day."

"When did this happen?" I said.

"Not long ago. Maybe a week. The next day, he gave me this. He asked me to keep it safe for him. He was always afraid someone would steal it from him. He said it was all he had." She opened her hand to reveal a ring and a small envelope. She opened the envelope and took out a small black-and-white photograph that had been trimmed into an oval shape. It was a picture of a boy, maybe sixteen or seventeen years old.

"Did he say who this is?" I said.

Aisha shook her head. "But it looks very old. I thought at first it was a picture of him, but it doesn't look anything like him."

It sure didn't. But then, this was the picture of a

boy, and Mr. Duffy had been over sixty years old when he died, according to the coroner's estimate, and was grizzled and scarred with one twisted eye. Morgan took the picture from me and peered at it.

"Some things never change," she said.

I looked at her. "What do you mean?"

"School pictures," she said. "They're like driver's licence photos and passport photos. You always come out looking like either a geek or a criminal. This guy's definitely a geek — check the outfit." Even though the picture was small — just head and shoulders — we could see that he was wearing a white shirt, a jacket, and a tie.

Aisha handed me the ring. It was a school ring. The words *St. Mark's Academy* were inscribed on it. There was no date.

"You can take these," Aisha said. "Maybe they will help you."

I slipped the ring and the small envelope into my bag. Morgan and I put on our boots and warm coats while Aisha tidied up the tea things and retied the string on the box that contained the remaining cupcakes.

"Aisha?" I said. I held out the bag from the toy store — a gift for Yasmin. Aisha peeked into it but shook her head. I didn't argue with her. She handed me the box of cupcakes.

"But the cupcakes are for you," Morgan protested.

I took the box from Aisha. "Thanks for your help," I said. "We really appreciate it." I fumbled in my purse until I found a piece of paper and a pen. I wrote down my phone number and handed it to her. "If there's anything I can do — if you need someone to babysit Yasmin, anything at all — call me. I mean it."

She nodded and folded the piece of paper, then tucked it into her pocket. "If you find out anything about Mr. Duffy, will you tell me?" she said.

I promised I would.

When we were outside again, Morgan said, "Now what?"

I looked down at the ring and the small envelope.

Chapter 11

Morgan and I parted company. She was going home. I was heading over to my father's place, but I decided to make a stop along the way.

The staff and volunteers at the drop-in centre were gearing up for another out-of-the-cold night. They were busy setting up rows of cots and laying out blankets and pillows in the main hall. The place was more crowded than usual. I had to thread my way through people and bedding to get to the far end of the hall where I'd spotted Mr. Donovan talking to a client.

"Robyn," he said when he had finished his conversation. "I've already told Ben and now I'm going to tell you."

"Tell me what?"

"That what you and Ben have been doing has resulted in some generous donations to the drop-in centre."

"Really?" I had already given him the wad of twenties that the man outside the office building had given me.

"I received a thousand-dollar donation from a judge," he said. "And a man — a Mr. Franklin — wrote us an even bigger cheque. He mentioned you by name and said he thought what you were doing was admirable." I recognized the name. It was the man who had given me his business card and had told Ben and me to let him know if we ever solved our 'little mystery.' After hearing about his donation, I promised myself that I would do just that.

"That's great," I said. "Mr Donovan, I was wondering — "

"Excuse me," someone said. It was a volunteer who was preparing to set up a couple more cots.

"We'd better step into my office," Mr. Donovan said.

We had to squeeze through more people to get there. Cots filled the main hall now, and some had already been claimed. I was surprised by how many faces I recognized: Andrew, some of the men I'd seen outside smoking, the man who always wore all of his clothes rather than risk being robbed again, the man with the black tuque from the funeral, even Aggie, who scowled at me and muttered something angrily under her breath. She still hadn't forgiven me for contradicting her.

We went into Mr. Donovan's office, but he left the door ajar so that he could keep an eye on the proceedings.

"What can I do for you, Robyn?"

I handed him the little oval photograph that Aisha had given me and watched as he studied it.

"Am I supposed to recognize this boy?" he said.

"Do you?" I said.

He examined the photo again. "You don't by any chance want me to say this looks like a young Mr. Duffy, do you?"

I felt a small surge of excitement. "Do you think it does?"

He shook his head slowly. "I'm sorry, but not to me it doesn't."

"And you've never seen this picture before?" I said.

"No."

"What about this ring?" I showed it to him. He shook his head again.

"I'm sorry, Robyn. I've never seen either of them before."

I had been hoping for a different answer, but I hadn't really been expecting one.

Betty gave me the same response. I looked around the main hall for Andrew.

"Do you recognize these?" I said and showed him the small oval-shaped photograph and the ring.

He inspected both items and shook his head. When he saw the look on my face, he gave me a sympathetic look. "Wrong answer, huh?"

"Well, it wasn't the one I was hoping for. Someone gave me these. They belonged to Mr. Duffy. I thought maybe they meant something." I glanced around. The place was really filling up now. I wondered what the chances were that Mr. Duffy had shown the photo and the ring to anyone else.

"Do you want me to ask around for you?" Andrew said in his soft, mumbly voice. "People might tell me things that they wouldn't tell you."

"Would you?"

He started to smile, but quickly hid his mouth with his hand again.

He took the ring and the photo and began a circuit of the room. I watched him. He spoke to everyone — the smokers, Aggie, the man with the black tuque, even the volunteers who were handing out blankets and pillows. Mostly I saw heads shaking in response to what he was saying. A few times, the person he was talking to turned and looked at me. Then, suddenly, a man grabbed the ring out of Andrew's hand and bolted for the door. Andrew ran after him. I ran after Andrew but stopped just outside the front door. Andrew had caught up with the man and was arguing with him. The man looked over Andrew's shoulder at me. It was the man with the mismatched eyes. He glowered at me just as he'd done the time I'd tried to ask him about Mr. Duffy. I heard Andrew mention the police. The man swore, but he thrust the ring at Andrew and stalked away. Andrew turned to come back inside.

"I don't like that guy," he said. "He's crazy, and he's always trying to take people's stuff."

We went back inside, and Andrew continued where he had left off. When he had finally spoken to every person in the room, he said, "Nobody knows anything." He looked and sounded more disappointed than I was.

"Thanks for asking," I said. I slipped the ring and the photo into my coat pocket and said good night.

As usual, there was a small group of men on the sidewalk in front of the drop-in centre. As usual, most of them were smoking what looked like hand-rolled cigarettes. And, as usual, they ignored me — all except for the man with the mismatched eyes. He stared at me as I came down the steps. He looked fierce, but I told myself that it was his strange eyes that gave him that appearance. I wrapped my hand around the ring and walked past him. As I started up the street for the bus stop, one of the centre's vans turned into the church parking lot and unloaded more clients. Eileen got out with them. I doubled back and showed her the picture. She just shook her head. With a sigh, I headed back to the sidewalk. On my way, I passed the man in the black tuque who had been at the funeral. I realized then that I had been wrong about him — he must have been a volunteer, not a client, because he got into a car and drove up the street past me.

The bus shelter was empty when I got there. It was dark and cold out, and I was tired and hungry. I glanced at my watch and then at the bus schedule posted inside the shelter. Great. I had just missed a bus and would have to wait ten minutes for the next one. I hugged myself and stamped my feet to stay warm.

Someone stepped into the bus shelter with me. It

was the man with the mismatched eyes. He stared at me with his one good eye. Was he still after the ring? Did he think he could get it away from me now that I was all alone?

I closed my hand protectively around the ring and the photograph in my pocket and glanced nervously up and down the street, hoping to see someone, anyone, approaching the bus shelter. It didn't matter who, just so long as I wasn't alone.

There was no one in sight.

The man kept staring at me.

At first I turned away and ignored him. Then he moved closer to me. I felt myself tense up. He moved even closer, blocking my exit. I saw the clouds of his breath in my peripheral vision. I decided to get out of there.

"Excuse me," I said. The man didn't move. I darted around behind him, squeezed out of the bus shelter, and walked quickly away. I told myself to stay calm. Andrew had said that the guy was crazy, but he hadn't said that he was dangerous. Maybe he was really just waiting for the bus. Maybe he wasn't following me. I glanced around.

He was following me.

I walked a little faster.

I could hear his footsteps quicken behind me.

I glanced over my shoulder again. He was right behind me, and there was no one else around.

I spotted a car coming in my direction. A car with a lit dome on the roof. A taxi.

I raised a hand to flag it down.

It pulled over and I jumped in.

"Where to?" the taxi driver said.

I gave him my father's address.

* * *

When the taxi pulled up in front of my father's building, I told the taxi driver that I would be right back, that I needed to get some money. But when I got out, the driver jumped out, too, and grabbed me by the arm. Maybe he hadn't understood me. Or maybe he was afraid I was trying to get away without paying him.

"I'll be right back," I told him again. But he wouldn't let me go.

Fortunately, Lauren, the hostess at La Folie, spotted me out on the sidewalk and went to get my father, who was occupying his usual table for dinner. He ran out into the frigid night without a coat or even a jacket and paid my fare. Then he shepherded me back into the restaurant, where he had been enjoying an after-dinner cognac with his business partner Vern Deloitte.

"We were just talking about you, Robyn," Vern said when I approached the table with my father.

"You were?"

"Mac told me all about that homeless man who froze to death," Vern said. "Sounds like you've been doing some good works. This is the season for it."

I nodded distractedly. I felt shaky all over and I couldn't stop myself from turning to look outside. I kept expecting to see the man with mismatched eyes.

"Robbie, are you okay?" my father said.

"Huh?"

He was staring intently at me. "You keep looking out the window. And you're shaking like a leaf."

"There was this man," I said. "He was following me. That's why I took a taxi over here."

My father's expression turned grim. "What man?" he said. "And what do you mean, he was following you?" He got up, unbuttoned my coat for me, and pulled it off. That's when I realized that my hand was still clenched around the ring and the small photo. I put them on the table and pulled off my gloves.

"I think he wanted this ring. He tried to steal it when Andrew was showing it around the drop-in centre."

My father looked at the ring and the photo, and frowned. "I think you'd better back up, Robbie. Whose ring is this, who is Andrew, and why was he showing it around?"

"Andrew is a regular at the drop-in centre. He was showing it around to see if anyone had seen it before. Mr. Duffy gave it to someone for safekeeping. I was trying to find out if it was a picture of him."

"The man who froze to death," my father said to Vern.

Vern turned the photo around to look at it. He glanced across the table at my father, his expression serious now, too. Two ex-cops, their antennae up.

"Tell me about the man who followed you," my father said.

"After Andrew caught him and made him give back the ring, he followed me to the bus stop," I said.

"He kept staring at me. He was making me nervous, so I started to walk away. He followed me again. That's when I flagged down a taxi." I realized I was nervous about nothing. "He was on foot," I said. "There's no way he could have followed me here. He scared me, Dad. But I'm okay now."

I sensed my father relaxing just a little. Vern drained the cognac from his glass and stood up.

"You want me to check the guy out, Mac?" he said.

My father shook his head. "I think Robbie's right. If he was on foot, he couldn't have followed her. I think we're in the clear for now."

"Okay," Vern said. "You take care of yourself, now, Robyn. And I think what you're doing is great. I mean it."

I thanked him. I really like Vern. He's kind of like an uncle to me. He's known me my whole life, and he's always as proud of me as my parents are.

"Call me if you need me, Mac," he said.

"Have you had dinner, Robbie?" my father said after Vern left.

I shook my head.

My father flagged down a waiter, and I ordered something to eat. While we waited, my father said, "Tell me again what happened."

I told him exactly how the ring and the photo had come into my possession, and how I had gone back to the drop-in centre to see if anyone recognized them. By the time I had finished my story, my heart had stopped pounding and my hands and feet no longer felt like blocks of ice. The waiter arrived with my food. As I tucked into it, my father picked up the ring and looked closely at it.

"It's a school ring," he said. "There used to be a St. Mark's Academy here in town. It was a boys' school."

"Used to be? You mean it doesn't exist anymore?" I had been hoping the school would be able to help me find out something about Mr. Duffy — assuming he had ever been a student there.

"It went co-ed about twenty years ago and changed its name. I think it's called the Ashdale Academy now."

Ashdale Academy?

"But Ashdale is an all-boys' school, Dad."

"The co-ed thing didn't work out. It reverted to boys-only after a couple of years. You're sure this belonged to Mr. Duffy?"

"He gave it and the photo to Aisha for safe-keeping," I said. "So they must have meant something to him."

My father examined the small photograph. "That's kind of an old-fashioned haircut. And that tie . . . I'd say this was taken forty, maybe fifty years ago. You think it could be Mr. Duffy when he was young?"

"I was hoping," I said. "But no one who knew Mr. Duffy sees any resemblance."

"It's cut in an odd shape, don't you think?"

I had wondered about the shape. It looked like someone had trimmed it — maybe to fit a locket.

A cell phone rang. My father's.

"Excuse me a minute, Robbie."

"No problem." The truth was, I wanted to make a call myself. I pulled out my own phone and punched in Ben's number. He sounded surprised to hear from me. He sounded even more surprised when I asked him if there was any chance his school was open next week or if it had already closed for the holidays.

"It's closed," he said. When I sounded disappointed, he said, "What I mean is, classes are over, and most of the teachers are probably gone. But I know there are still a few people around. I'm going over there tomorrow morning to pick up some stuff for the toy drive."

"Toy drive?"

"Ashdale and another school do a joint toy drive every year — you know, for underprivileged kids. I'm supposed to pick up the toys Ashdale collected and take them to the other school for the wrap-a-thon."

"Wrap-a-thon, huh?" That was a new one on me. "Do you think anyone will be in the office?"

"Well, I know Mr. Thorson is going to be there. He's the headmaster. Why?"

"What time are you going?"

"First thing."

"Can I meet you?"

"What's going on, Robyn?"

"I think I may have a lead, Ben. At least, I hope so. I'll show you tomorrow."

We agreed to meet in front of Ben's school at nine the next morning.

After I put my phone away, I ate every bite of my supper and told my father what Morgan and I had found out so far about Mr. Duffy. I felt warm and relaxed and safe.

"I'm impressed," he said, smiling at me. "Don't tell your mother, but if you ever decided to go into policing, you'd make detective in no time. You're a natural."

I grinned. "Everything I learned, I learned from you, Dad."

"Don't tell your mother that, either."

His cell phone rang again.

"Tara," he said into it, sounding pleased. "No, don't apologize. What can I do for you?"

Tara? If he was making plans with her, I didn't want to get in the way.

"I gotta go, Dad." I stood up.

"Just a moment," my father said into the phone. Then he looked up at me. "Go? Go where?"

"Home."

My father gave me an odd look. "Home?" he said. "I thought you were staying here tonight."

I glanced at his phone. "I left something . . . um . . . I should go home, Dad." I scooped up the ring and the photograph and put them safely in my purse.

"Give me a minute and I'll drive you," my father said.

"It's okay. I can get home on my own."

"Well, at least let me give you cab fare." He pressed some bills into my hand. "Take a taxi. I insist. Have Lauren call one for you."

"Dad, stop worrying."

But I took the money and slipped on my coat while my father resumed his phone conversation. When I got to the front of the restaurant, Lauren was busy sorting out a problem with a large group of diners who had just arrived. I didn't want to bother her.

It was quiet out on the street. A couple of cars went by, but no taxis. I decided to walk down to the intersection where there was more traffic. I'd have a better chance of finding a cab there.

I was a block away from the restaurant when I felt a sharp jerk on my purse strap. Then the pressure stopped and my purse fell away from my shoulder. The strap had been cut. I started to turn around but was suddenly shoved into a dark alley. The person who had shoved me was wearing a balaclava so that I couldn't see his face. He was holding a knife. I stared at it and couldn't make myself look away. The knife was long and looked razor-sharp.

Chapter 12

I opened my mouth. I don't think I was going to scream. I'm pretty sure that I understood it would be crazy to make any noise at all under the circumstances. But I opened my mouth anyway, and I think that's what made him hit me. I fell to the ground, stunned but not unconscious. I felt rough hands on me, plunging into my pockets, groping inside them, pulling things out. Then he pushed me down again, on my stomach this time. I lay there for a moment, too frightened to move.

Nothing happened.

I peered around.

The man was gone.

I staggered to my feet. My cheek hurt from where he had hit me. I felt the bandage that hid my stitches, afraid that he had re-opened the wound. But it was dry. My cell phone lay on the ground at my feet. I picked it up and put it back into my pocket. The money my father had given me was gone. I wobbled back to La Folie.

My father was still talking on the phone, but he ended his call the moment he saw me. The expression on his face told me that I looked as shaky as I felt. I don't know how he got from his table to the foyer so quickly, but just like that, there he was. He put his arms around me and led me out the door and up the stairs to his place. He made me tell him everything. When I had finished, he made a phone call. It wasn't long before two uniformed police officers arrived, and my father made me tell them what I had already told him.

"What about that bandage on your face, is that from the man who robbed you?" one of the cops said.

I shook my head and explained.

"Do you think the man who robbed you outside the restaurant is the same man who followed you to the bus shelter?"

"I don't know. I didn't get a good look at him."

"He was wearing a balaclava," my father said grimly.

"What about the man from the bus shelter?" the same cop said. "Can you describe him?"

I nodded and told them everything I remembered about him. They wrote down the description and asked me some more questions about what I had seen when I left the restaurant. Then they closed their notebooks and stood up. My father followed them to the door and talked to them for a few minutes before they finally left.

"They're going to check out the guy who followed you to the bus shelter," my father said. He caught my chin in one hand and tilted my head back so that he could get a good look at me. "You're going to have a bruise," he said. His fog-grey eyes held mine. "I should have driven you to your mother's."

"When I saw that knife — "

"It's okay, Robbie. You're safe now." He reached for my coat. "Come on. I'll take you home."

"But what if the police find out something?"

"If they do, I'll let you know."

"What if they want to talk to me again?"

"Then *they'll* let you know."

"If they call me at Mom's — or worse, if they show up there — Mom will freak out. She'll never let me come down here alone again."

"Robbie, your mother has a right to know — "

"She's already been giving me a hard time about the drop-in centre. Please, Dad. I'm okay, really. We don't have to get her all upset, do we?"

He was still holding my coat, but he didn't try to help me into it.

"You have to tell her."

"She already knows I was planning to spend the night here."

"Didn't you say you left something at home?"

"It's not important," I said. "Please, Dad. You know how she can be."

My father hesitated.

"But you have to promise me that you'll tell her what happened when you see her," he said at last.

"When she sees that bruise — "

"I'll tell her, I promise. But not tonight, okay, Dad?"

Finally, reluctantly, he agreed.

* * *

I took a long, hot bath and then curled up on the couch and turned on the TV. I had almost given up hope of hearing from the police again that night when my father's buzzer sounded. He went to answer it. A few moments later, he opened the door and the same two police officers stepped in. One of them was holding my purse, its strap cut in half and dangling uselessly.

"Where did you find it?" I said.

"In an alley a couple of blocks away," he said. "That's pretty standard. Purse snatchers grab a purse and run like hell. When they think they're safe, they take everything of value and dump the purse. Your wallet's inside." I reached for the purse. The cop shook his head. "We're going to want to hold onto it for a while," he said. "It's evidence. Same for your wallet. We'll see if we can get some prints off them."

"But he was wearing gloves," I said. "The guy who attacked me was wearing gloves."

"Purse snatchers aren't exactly geniuses," the cop said. "You'd be surprised how many guys wear gloves when they're doing the crime and then do something stupid right after, like taking off the gloves so they can go through the purse more easily. It's always worth checking. We'll let you know if we find anything. I can give you back your ID — but you'll have to sign for it. Did you have any money in the wallet?"

I nodded.

"Well I hope it wasn't much because it's gone now," the cop said. "Any credit cards?"

I shook my head.

"Anything else of value?"

"There was a gold ring in the purse. And a photograph. Are they still there?"

The cop shook his head.

"Are you sure?"

"Positive. I inventoried the contents myself." He showed me the list he had written.

"There are other things missing," I said. "Some lipgloss. Some blusher."

"It's possible he tossed those," the cop said.

"Maybe he threw away the ring, too," I said. "Or the photo." What would a purse snatcher want with an old photo? "Where exactly did you find my purse?"

When he described the alley, my father nodded. "I know the one you mean."

"We found the purse about halfway down the alley," the cop said. "The place is a mess. It's possible your make-up is in there somewhere. Maybe the picture, too. But a gold ring? I doubt it, but we can take another look."

"It's okay," my father said. "I'll do it myself."

The cop nodded. He reached into his pocket and pulled out a Polaroid photo. "Is this the guy who followed you from the drop-in centre to the bus stop?"

I looked at the man in the photo. He had one dark eye and one milky white eye.

"That's him."

"Well, he wasn't the guy who attacked you downstairs," the cop said. "The director at the drop-in centre says this guy went out for a smoke early in the evening — just about the time you left to walk to the bus stop. He was back fifteen minutes later and stayed inside for the rest of the night."

"He's sure about that?" my father said.

"He's positive. So is the woman who works in the kitchen. A bunch of other people at the centre say he was there all evening." The two cops stood up. "We're going to check your purse and wallet for prints. If we find any, we'll run them against what's in the system."

The second cop, the one who had stayed silent on both visits and had done most of the note taking, returned my student identification card, my health card, my library card, and my transit card. He made me sign for each item. Then the two cops left.

"How about a cup of tea?" my father said.

I slipped on my boots and my coat. "How about showing me where that alley is?"

"Robyn, it's nearly midnight. Whatever's there is going to stay there, believe me."

"Please, Dad? If the ring is there, I don't want to take the chance that someone will find it. It could be important. You don't have to go with me if you don't want to." But I sure hoped that he *would* want to. I didn't want to go back to that alley by myself tonight.

"Just tell me where it is." I buttoned my jacket and pulled on my gloves.

My father sighed and stood up. "You are so stubborn," he said. "Sometimes I don't know who you remind me more of — your mother or me."

He pulled on his own boots and coat and got a couple of flashlights out of a drawer. We trudged down the street to the alley the two police officers had described and spent nearly an hour hunting through the trash cans, discarded boxes, and assorted litter. I found my blusher. My father found my lipgloss. But we didn't find the ring or the photo. Neither of us was surprised. But one of us was more disappointed than the other.

* * *

After a nearly sleepless night, I met Ben, as arranged, the next morning. He was waiting for me on the sidewalk in front of a modern-looking building in one of the most upscale parts of the city. The weather hadn't changed. It was still bone-shatteringly cold out. I had a hat pulled down over my ears and had wrapped a thick wool scarf around and around my neck and over my chin to stay warm. I stared up at the glass-and-steel structure.

"*This* is Ashdale Academy?" I said. I had heard of it, but I had never seen it.

"What were you expecting? Gothic towers and ivory-covered walls?"

"Something like that," I admitted. For sure I had been expecting something that looked a lot older. "My dad must have made a mistake. He said that this school used to be called St. Mark's."

"It did."

"Well, there must be more than one, because the school I'm looking for was around at least forty or fifty years ago." If Mr. Duffy had gone there, it would have been much, much older than the school I was staring at now. "This place looks like it was built much more recently."

"It was," Ben said. "This building was supposed to be an addition to the original St. Mark's."

"Supposed to be?"

"There was a fire," Ben said. "Shortly after the new wing was built."

"A fire?" That didn't sound promising.

"They had to knock down the old building completely and expand the new addition. My father helped to raise the money for it. What are we doing here, Robyn? You said you had a lead on Mr. Duffy. Does it have something to do with St. Mark's?"

When I'd told him the night before that I had a lead, I had imagined presenting him with the photo and the ring. But they were long gone. All I could do was tell him about them instead.

"Great work," he said. "Can I see them?"

"I'm afraid not. They were stolen."

His eyes widened. "Stolen?"

"I was mugged last night."

"*Mugged?* Were you hurt?"

I turned my head and pulled down my scarf so he could see the bruise on my face.

His eyes widened even more. "Are you okay?"

"I'm fine." At least I was *now*. I had thought I was fine at my father's last night, too, after the police left. But I'd had trouble falling asleep. I had tossed and turned and twisted the sheets into knots. I kept thinking about that knife.

"Did you call the police? Did they catch the guy who mugged you?"

"Yes," I said. "And no, they didn't. Not yet, anyway."

"You think the ring means that Mr. Duffy used to go to St. Mark's?" he said.

It was hard to imagine, but, "Maybe. Or maybe somebody important to him did. I'm not sure. But he told Aisha that he didn't want to lose the ring or the picture, and so they must have been valuable to him."

I shivered as a gust of wind hit me.

"Do you think we could go inside?" I said.

Ben nodded. He led the way up the walk and rang a bell beside the front door. I peered inside. The school looked deserted except for a man who was mopping the floor just inside the main doors. He looked up when he heard the buzzer and came and opened the door for us.

"Hi, Pete," Ben said as he stood aside to let me go in first.

"Ben, didn't they tell you?" Pete said, grinning at him. "School's out for the holidays."

"I'm here to pick up the toys for the toy drive," Ben said.

Pete gestured to a huge pile of cardboard cartons stacked to one side of the foyer.

"I'll go and get a dolly," he said. "It'll go faster that way."

"Thanks," Ben said. "I'll meet you back here in a few minutes. I need to talk to Mr. Thorson. Have you seen him?"

"Who do you think packed all those boxes?" Pete said. "He's in the office."

"Come on," Ben said.

I followed him down the hallway to the school's administrative offices, which, like the rest of the school, were silent and empty. Well, almost empty.

"Ben," said the office's sole occupant, a smiling, bald-headed man dressed casually in grey slacks and a grey pullover sweater. He seemed as delighted to see Ben as Pete had been. "I put all the toys in the foyer for you. Do you need help loading them up?"

"Pete's going to help me," Ben said. "But thanks anyway, Mr. Thorson."

Mr. Thorson's eyes moved from Ben to me and back to Ben again. Ben took the hint and introduced me.

"Robyn and I were hoping you could give us some information, sir," he said. "Robyn found a ring that she thinks might be from this school — from when it used to be St. Mark's."

"Indeed. May I see it?" Mr. Thorson said.

"I don't have it anymore," I said. "It was stolen last night."

"Oh?"

"But I can describe it," I said. I told him everything I could remember about the ring. But it wasn't until I did a rough sketch of the crest that appeared on its face that he started to nod. He got up, went to the wall behind his desk, and removed a framed certificate.

"Did it look like this?" he said, pointing to the crest that was embossed on the heavy certificate paper.

"Exactly," I said.

"Then it sounds as though it was a St. Mark's school ring," Mr. Thorson said. "As I understand it, that was the ring from the time the school opened until it changed its name, and that's twenty years ago now. I started as headmaster here that same year."

So my father had been right after all. And if this was the right school, there was a chance that Mr. Duffy had been a student here. If he had, there would be records somewhere that could tell us something about him. Assuming, of course . . .

"Ben said the original school burned down," I said.

"That's right. Quite spectacularly," Mr. Thorson said. "A pity, too. The original building was over one hundred years old. We were able to incorporate some of what was left of the old structure into the new building — a blend of the old and the new, bridging generations, as it were. Fortunately the new building was completed and renovations were just about to begin on the old structure, so we were able to carry on without missing a beat."

"What about the school records?" I said.

"We only lost the old records — everything dating back more than ten years before the new school opened," Mr. Thorson said.

My heart sank. "We were hoping there would be records on whoever the ring belonged to," I said.

"How old was he?" Mr. Thorson said.

"Sixty, maybe sixty-five."

Mr. Thorson shook his head. "I'm afraid anything that dates from that era is long gone."

Great.

"Was there a date on the ring, Robyn?" Ben said.

I shook my head.

"The St. Mark's school rings didn't have dates on them," Mr. Thorson said. "The graduation rings, which did, were of a different design. From the description you just gave me, I'd say that what you had was a school ring, not a graduation ring. Every boy who went to St. Mark's received one. There must be thousands of them in existence. As I understand it, the design of that ring never changed."

In other words, there was no way to trace it to a specific graduating class, let alone a specific student.

"What about the photo?" Ben said.

"What photo?" Mr. Thorson said.

"I had a photo of a boy," I said. "It looked like a school photo. It was stolen along with the ring. But I'm pretty sure I'd recognize the face if I saw it again." That gave me an idea, but before I could say anything, Mr. Thorson shook his head.

"You're thinking that if you looked through old yearbooks, you might be able to find the same face."

That was exactly what I had been thinking.

"I'm sorry, Robyn," Mr. Thorson said. "But that won't be possible, either."

"You mean there are no yearbooks?" Ben said, disappointed.

"Only Ashdale yearbooks. All the St. Mark's yearbooks are long gone," Mr. Thorson said.

"Were they burned in the fire, too?" I said.

"They were water-damaged — in a separate incident, believe it or not," Mr. Thorson said. "They were stored in the basement of the new school, this building you're standing in now. We had some problems with the pipes the first year. The basement flooded. Everything down there, including our collection of old yearbooks, which was supposed to have ended up in the school library, was utterly destroyed. We were hoping some of our alumni would donate their personal copies so that we could rebuild our collection, but — " He shrugged. "I guess after a fire and a flooded basement, they didn't want to take any chances."

"So there's no way we can find out who the ring belonged to or whether the boy in the photo was a student here?"

Mr. Thorson looked genuinely apologetic. "I'm sorry," he said.

I was even sorrier.

* * *

I helped Ben and Pete load the boxes of toys into the van Ben was driving. Then Ben dropped me at the bus stop before delivering the toys to their next destination.

"I thought we really were on to something there for a while," Ben said as I reached for the door handle to let myself out. "Talk about bad luck, huh?"

"Well, it was worth a try," I said.

I went back to my father's place. It was still early. Morgan wouldn't be up yet, so I planned to just chill until it was time to go out again. I had promised to help out at the drop-in centre in the afternoon.

When I unlocked the door, I heard music coming from my father's office.

"Dad?" I dropped my coat and my bag on a chair and went to see what he was doing.

He wasn't in the office, but Tara was. She was working on my father's computer and was so immersed in what she was doing that she didn't even seem to notice that I was there. I knocked on the door to get her attention. She jumped and spun around in her chair as if I'd jabbed her with a pin.

"Robyn," she said, her hand pressed to her chest. "You startled me."

"I was looking for my dad," I said. I stared at the computer screen and at the image that filled most of it. It was my mother's face. I crossed to the desk so that I could take a closer look. There was something weird about it. It was definitely my mother, but it was like no picture of her that I had ever seen. I couldn't put my finger on exactly what was wrong with it. It just seemed off.

"Mac said he had to meet somebody," Tara said. She glanced at her watch and seemed surprised at the time. "No wonder I'm hungry." She looked at me again. "I tend to get a little too involved in what I'm doing."

"What *are* you doing?" I said. What I really meant:

Why is my mother's face on the computer you're working on? Supplementary question: Whatever you're doing, why are you doing it in my father's office?

"I'm working on age progression. My computer crashed, oh, two weeks ago now. It's still in the shop. Can you believe it? Anyway, your father was nice enough to offer me the use of his — which, by the way, is ten times better than my old hunk of junk."

"Age progression? You mean, like the police do when they're trying to find some kid who disappeared years ago?"

"Missing kids, criminals who are at large, you name it." She nodded at the computer screen. "I've been practising on some photos your father gave me, pictures of people he knows." She fumbled around on the desk until she found a photograph that I recognized instantly. It was a school picture of my mother, from when she was about ten years old. She showed me another photo — a geeky-looking Ted, age maybe thirteen or fourteen, which explained the image of him that I had seen on my father's computer the first time I had met Tara. I wondered where my father had got the picture and if my mother knew that he had it. "I've been ageing them, and your father has been able to tell me how well I'm doing because he knows what they look like now."

"Are you a cop?"

"I'm an anthropologist. My area of expertise is human osteology. That's — "

"The study of human bones. I know."

She nodded. "Thanks to one of my former professors, I've done a little work for the police. You know, identifying bones, giving the police some idea of how old they are, that sort of thing. I found it interesting, so I've been taking some courses. Age progression fascinates me. It's a direction I've decided to go in."

"Oh." I looked at the image of my mother on the computer screen. "You and my father . . . Are you — " What was the right way to ask the question I had in mind?

Tara frowned. "Are we what?" Then a look of horror swept across her face. "You mean, are we . . . ? You think your father and I . . . " She shook her head vigorously. "I'm in town to take a course and do some hands-on study with a forensic artist here who's considered *the* expert in age progression and regression. Mac's been nice enough to show me around, and he offered me the use of his computer when mine crashed. But — " She seemed mortified at the thought that I had read more than that into the situation. "I mean, my God," she said. "I've known him my whole life as *Uncle* Mac. It's hard enough to get used to calling him just plain Mac, let alone . . . " She shook her head again.

"*Uncle* Mac?" I said. As far as I knew, I didn't have any cousins.

"Your dad and my dad worked together."

I looked at her with new interest. "Your dad's a *cop?*"

"He was," she said. Then, "He was killed in the line

of duty nearly twenty years ago."

That might explain why I didn't know her.

"I'm sorry," I said.

She shrugged. "I was seven when it happened. My mother completely fell apart. Your dad and some of the other cops who worked with my father used to come around to check on her, do things around the house for her, take my brother and me out, that kind of thing." She smiled. "I had more uncles than anyone I knew. And your father was the nicest one. He always kept in touch with Brad — that's my brother — and me, even after Mom remarried a few years later and moved us clear across the country. I think that's one of the reasons I'm interested in this area of work — I want to carry on the family tradition. Brad went in another direction. He didn't want anything at all to do with police work. He's a master carpenter."

I wondered why my father hadn't told me about Tara. Then I remembered what he'd said when I mentioned that she seemed a little young. "I think she's just about right," he had replied. Just about right to be the daughter of an old friend. He'd been having some fun with me, letting me think she was more than a friend. Maybe he'd been hoping I would tell my mother.

"I was going to make myself a cup of tea," I said. "Would you like one?"

Tara beamed at me. "I'd love one," she said.

On the way to the kitchen, I checked my father's phone. There were no messages. Still no word from Nick.

Chapter 13

The drop-in centre served a Christmas dinner every year that attracted more than two hundred and fifty homeless people. The dinner consisted of turkey, mashed potatoes, peas and carrots, bread-and-sage stuffing, gravy, rolls and butter, and, for dessert, pie and ice cream. A local bakery donated the pies. Everything else was made at the drop-in centre. Some of it — the gravy, the bread stuffing, and the potatoes — could be prepared ahead of time and either frozen or refrigerated. It was a lot of work. If Betty was going to be ready in time for Christmas, she would need all the help she could get. I hung up my coat, changed out of my boots and into a pair of sneakers, and went to the kitchen to see what she wanted me to do.

"Onions," Betty said. "I need someone to chop onions." She nodded at a large mesh bag that was sitting on the floor.

"How many do you need chopped?" I said.

168

Her answer didn't surprise me. "All of them."

I positioned myself near the sink. Proximity to a sink was, I knew, critical to successful onion chopping. I had learned this from Fred Smith, owner of La Folie. I had complained to him once how much I hated it when my mother made me chop onions. "I always end up with red eyes and tears streaming down my face," I'd told him.

"Run cold water over your wrists whenever your eyes start to water," he had advised. "Works like a charm. Guaranteed."

I'd tried it. It worked. Onions didn't faze me anymore.

I heaved the sack of onions up onto the counter beside my cutting board and set to work. To my surprise, a few minutes later, Andrew set up beside me to cut day-old loaves of bread into small cubes for the stuffing.

"Hey, Robyn," he said, smiling at me without showing his teeth.

"Hey, Andrew," I said. "Don't tell me they're making you work for your supper."

"I volunteered," he said. He looked proud of himself. "It's the thing to do this time of year, right?"

"Right," I said. Once again I wondered what had drawn Andrew to the street. And once again I hesitated to ask.

"Wow, that's a lot of onions," said a voice behind me. I whirled around. It was Ben. He was carrying a stack of bakery boxes. "Where do you want me to put these, Betty?"

"I cleared out some space in one of the downstairs freezers," Betty said. "We'll freeze them until Christmas Eve. Then we'll take them out and warm them in the oven as needed on Christmas Day. Robyn, do you think you could help Ben with those?"

I was glad to.

"You didn't tell me *you* were coming here today," I said.

"You didn't tell me you were coming."

It took us two trips to get all the pies downstairs and neatly stacked in one of the centre's two mammoth chest freezers. There were forty boxes in all — twenty apple pies and twenty cherry pies. After we had finished, Ben helped me finish chopping onions and, under Betty's directions, we mixed a huge batch of bread stuffing, which we then packed in plastic containers and set into the freezer with the pies. When we'd done everything that Betty had on her schedule for the day, Ben offered to drive me home.

* * *

"You live *here?*" he said. We were sitting in his car outside my father's place.

"My dad does. Why?"

"La Folie is supposed to be a really good restaurant. My dad comes here a lot. Does your father own it?"

I shook my head. "He owns the building but not the restaurant."

"So he's in real estate?"

"He has his own business. Private security. He used to be a cop."

Ben looked impressed. "My father manufactures and sells bathroom fixtures," he said, and shook his head. "It must be pretty exciting having a dad who's a cop."

"*Was* a cop," I said. "He was hardly ever home when I was little. He was always working. And when he was home, he hardly ever talked about what he did. So it wasn't really all that exciting."

"Yeah, well, my dad *does* talk about his business," Ben said. "Believe me, I know more about bathroom fixtures than I want to know — more than a person should ever have to know. So, Billy told me you got arrested in the summer. Something about an animal rights protest."

"I got arrested trying to stop *Billy* from getting arrested."

"Now *that* sounds exciting."

"Obviously you've never been arrested."

"I've never even known anyone who's been arrested." He smiled at me. "Boy, was I ever wrong about you. I thought you were like all the other girls I've ever met, but you're not. You're not anything like the girls at St. Mildred's."

"That's the second time you've mentioned the girls at St. Mildred's. What gives? Do boys from Ashdale have an exclusive with girls from St. Mildred's?"

"St. Mildred's is our sister school," Ben said. "Apparently it was some big tradition for guys from St. Mark's to go out with girls from St. Mildred's. Now a lot of guys from Ashdale go out with girls from St. Mildred's."

"Rich boys dating rich girls, huh?"

Ben shrugged. "I guess so. My mother went to St. Mildred's. My father went to St. Mark's. They met while they were at school." My eyes must have lit up because he said, "I thought of that, too. But my dad is at least fifteen years younger than Mr. Duffy. Their pictures wouldn't be in the same yearbook. And that's assuming that the ring actually belonged to Mr. Duffy, which we don't know. He could have found it — or stolen it. Besides, you said the picture didn't look anything like him."

I sighed and pushed open the car door. "Thanks for the lift."

"Robyn?"

I turned back to look at him.

"You want to go out sometime? See a movie or something?"

"What?" I guess I sounded too surprised because Ben's face turned red and he stared at the steering wheel. "What I mean is, are you sure that's allowed?"

He looked blankly at me.

"I don't go to St. Mildred's," I said. "I don't even go to private school. The way you talk about those St. Mildred's girls, I thought they had dibs on you Ashdale boys. You know — like father, like son."

His expression turned grim. "I'm not anything like my father," he said. He looked down at the steering wheel again and drew in a deep breath. "So, how about it? You want to go out with me?"

"I'd like that," I said. I don't think I would have admitted it — especially not to Morgan — but I was really starting to like him. He was nice — well, he was if he didn't think you were a two-four. He was cute. He cared about other people. And he didn't seem like the kind of person who would take off without any warning. I dug in my purse for paper and a pen and wrote out my phone number for him. "Call me," I said as I got out of the car. I had just turned to go into my father's building when a thought occurred to me. I ran back to the car and knocked on the window until Ben opened it. "Girls from St. Mildred's and boys from Ashdale, do they go out with each other because they already know each other?"

"Sometimes," Ben said. "Why?"

"If they don't already know each other, how do they get together?"

"What do you mean?"

"I mean, how do they meet each other?"

Ben shrugged. "Through mutual acquaintances. School events. You know, the same way anyone meets anyone else."

"My school is co-ed. Guys meet girls in class or in clubs or just in the hallways."

Ben laughed. "Okay, so obviously we don't meet that way. People just meet people — you know, through mutual acquaintances or just around. Plus, our schools have some joint social events, just like they did in the old days — although not exactly for the same reasons."

"What do you mean?"

"My mother told me that in her mother's time, and even in her time, St. Mark's and St. Mildred's used to organize dances and social events specifically so that girls from St. Mildred's would meet boys from St. Mark's — object: matrimony. You should see the pictures in both her and my father's yearbooks. They're filled with guys in suits arm in arm with girls in formal dresses."

I knew exactly the kind of picture he was talking about. Every high school yearbook I had ever seen included pages and pages of pictures just like that.

And that gave me an idea.

"St. Mildred's didn't ever burn down, did it, Ben?"

"Not that I know of."

"Did the basement ever flood?"

"Where are you going with this, Robyn?" When I told him my idea, he slapped his forehead. "I should have thought of that," he said.

I glanced at my watch. "You think there'd be anyone at St. Mildred's now?"

Ben shook his head. "I doubt it." When I looked disappointed, he said, "But there will be on Monday. And I can get us in."

"You can?"

He grinned. "I'll pick you up."

* * *

I spent the next day doing what Morgan liked to do best — Christmas shopping. By the end of the day, we had both checked off almost everyone on our lists.

"Who do you have left?" she said.

"My mother," I said. She was always the last person on my list because I never knew what to get her, and she never gave me any hints.

"What about Nick? What did you get him?"

I felt a twinge of anger.

"Nothing," I said. "What would I do with a present if I got him one? Where would I send it?"

"Still no word, huh?"

"Don't you think I would have told you, Morgan?" I said. Then, "I'm sorry. I didn't mean to snap at you. It's not your fault."

* * *

Ben picked me up just before noon, and we drove to St. Mildred's.

"Are you sure someone will be there?" I asked on the way.

"I'm positive. I'm supposed to help deliver all the wrapped toys to the children's organization we sponsor."

"You're supposed to go to St. Mildred's to pick up toys that students at *Ashdale* collected?" Now I was confused.

"Remember I told you that Ashdale does the toy drive every year with another school? Well, we do it with St. Mildred's. It's a tradition with the students and the alumni of both schools. I brought the toys Ashdale collected here yesterday and spent a couple of hours wrapping them."

We tried the main door. It was locked. Ben pressed the buzzer and we shivered as we waited for someone to answer.

Nothing happened.

I glanced at Ben, who rocked back and forth on his feet, humming quietly to himself.

Still nothing happened.

Ben continued to rock and hum.

Then I saw someone inside the school foyer. A man in work overalls. He shuffled toward the main door and peered out. He broke into a smile when he saw Ben and reached for a massive key ring that was attached to his belt. He looked familiar.

"Isn't that Pete, the janitor from *your* school?" I said to Ben.

"Yeah. He works at both Ashdale and St. Mildred's."

"Hey, Ben," Pete said, pushing the door open to admit us. We stepped into a richly panelled entrance hall. "Come back to help the ladies?"

"Are they still here?" Ben said.

"They're almost finished. They'll be ready to pack everything up soon," Pete said.

"That's why I'm here," Ben said.

"They're in the library."

"Thanks, Pete," Ben said. "You remember my friend Robyn?" Pete glanced at me and nodded. "She's helping me with something to do with Mr. Duffy. We want to look at old school yearbooks while we're here."

Pete looked confused. "What's Duffy got to do with yearbooks?"

"We're not sure," Ben said. "We're not even sure we're on the right track. But if we find out anything, we'll let you know."

Ben seemed to know the school well. He led me to the library.

"From the way Pete talked," I said, "I got the impression he knew Mr. Duffy."

"He did," Ben said. "Up until a few months ago, Pete was homeless. I met him at the drop-in centre."

Oh? "And now he's a janitor at your school and here at St. Mildred's," I said. "Coincidence?"

Ben shrugged. "Pete had some problems in the past. He was sick. You know, mentally ill. Because of that, his whole life fell apart and he ended up on the street. Things were pretty tough for him for a few years. When I met him, he was trying to get back on his feet. He was taking some job readiness courses at one of the community centres. He has a degree in chemistry."

"Really?"

"You're surprised, right?"

It would have been more accurate to say that I was stunned. I was as surprised to find out that Pete had a university degree as I had been to learn that Mr. Duffy read Dickens and computer magazines. I was beginning to think that I needed to be more open-minded about people.

"He worked hard to get into university," Ben said. "He worked hard while he was there. Now he's working hard to get it all back. When I met him, he was willing to do anything, anything at all, to make enough money so that he could get his own place and start to get his life together again. So when I heard that Ashdale was looking for a part-time janitor — " He shrugged again.

"You helped him get the job?" I said.

"I talked to Mr. Thorson. He knew I was volunteering at the drop-in centre. He said he'd interview Pete if he applied for the job but that he couldn't make any promises. Pete did really well in the interview. Mr. Thorson was impressed. He even arranged for Pete to audit some lectures at the university — you know, so he could start to get back on his original career track. And when St. Mildred's needed someone part-time, Mr. Thorson put in a word for him. Two part-time jobs — "

" — equal one full-time job," I said. No wonder Pete always seemed so delighted to see Ben — he was such a nice guy. He treated everyone with respect — well, everyone except the people he called two-fours.

Ben opened the library door and immediately a dozen heads turned in our direction. Several library tables had been pushed together and their entire surfaces were stacked with brightly wrapped Christmas gifts that a group of women were now busy packing into large cardboard boxes, also decorated with Christmas gift wrap.

"Hi, Ben," someone called. It was a girl who seemed to be about our age. She was dressed in casual but expensive-looking clothes. The moment she spotted Ben, she hurried over to greet him, calling back over her shoulder, "Mom, Ben's here."

"Jess, hi," Ben said. Jess threw her arms around him and kissed him on both cheeks. Ben didn't look the least bit embarrassed. When Jess finally released him, he introduced me. Jess tossed me a "Hi" but didn't take her eyes off Ben for a second. "Jess is president of the student council at St. Mildred's," Ben said. "She's in charge of the toy drive."

A woman came over to us. She was as sleek as Jess but more elegantly dressed.

"Ben, right on time," she said warmly. "We're just finishing up." Her eyes flicked over me, and once again Ben introduced me. She greeted me politely but coolly and then turned to her daughter. "Let's start taking the boxes out to Ben's van."

"Come on, Ben," Jess said. She looped one of her arms through one of his and smiled up at him.

"I'll be right back," Ben said to me. "This won't take long."

Instead of just standing around, I offered to help and followed Ben and Jess over to a table that was piled high with boxes, where another woman greeted Ben warmly.

"I heard you were here yesterday, Ben, and I was sorry I missed you," this woman said. She reached for an enormous handbag and immediately began to root around in it. Finally, she produced a small bundle of what looked like brochures. "We're raising money for a new computer lab," she said. "We've recruited one of our alumnae to be honorary chair of our fundraising committee. I was thinking that your father might be interested in this project. After all, your mother was a St. Mildred's graduate, wasn't she?" Ben nodded, but he no longer looked cheerful. "I wonder if you would mind giving this to your father," she said. "It's about the fundraising appeal.

Tell him I would be happy to discuss it with him after the holidays."

Ben accepted a brochure but stuffed it into his pocket without even glancing at it. He seemed relieved when Jess's mother clapped her hands to get everyone's attention.

"All right, everyone," she announced. "Let's load up and get out of here."

The women all pulled on coats and boots, and we each grabbed a box of toys. Pete joined us. The students and alumni at St. Mildred's and Ashdale had collected and wrapped so many toys that it took three trips to load everything into Ben's van. Jess stuck close to Ben the whole time, her brown eyes sparkling as she chatted with him about her plans for Christmas and New Year's and mentioned names that meant nothing to me but that clearly meant something to Ben. He responded affably. It was obvious that he knew Jess very well. When we had loaded the last of the boxes into the van and Jess's mother had climbed into her luxury SUV, Jess went up on tiptoes and kissed Ben again, on one cheek this time.

"See you at Stephanie's," she said.

Ben's face turned red.

"It's not what you think," he said, turning to me as Jess's mother's SUV pulled out of the parking lot.

"I wasn't thinking anything," I said, which wasn't entirely true. In fact, I had been thinking about all those St. Mildred's girls ending up with all those St. Mark's boys.

"Jess and I are just friends," he said.

"Okay," I said, trying to sound like it didn't matter to me one way or the other. Secretly, though, I was pleased. "Come on," I said. "We're here for a reason, remember?"

We went back into the library, and Ben led me to a shelf that was filled with identically bound books — the collection of St. Mildred's yearbooks.

"You really know your way around this place," I said. I wondered just how much time he had spent in St. Mildred's library — and with whom.

"I come here every now and again," he said.

"To hang out with Jess and Stephanie?" I was surprised that I even cared.

"To look at yearbooks."

That was hardly the answer I had expected.

When Ben saw the look on my face, he said, "That's why I should have thought of this."

"Do you mind if I ask why you'd come here to look at yearbooks?" I said.

He studied me for a moment, as if he were trying to decide what to say or even if he wanted to answer.

"My mother walked out on us when I was eight years old," he said at last. "She just packed a suitcase and left. She was sick."

"Sick?"

"Like Pete."

Oh. I couldn't imagine how it must have felt to lose someone — his mother — like that.

"I'm sorry," I said.

Ben just shrugged. "After she left, my dad threw

out all of her stuff, everything she had left behind. And I mean everything — her clothes, her books, pictures, her old school stuff. It was like he blamed her for being sick, you know? Then one day a couple of years ago I happened to be here."

"For one of those famous Ashdale–St. Mildred's social events?" I said.

"Not exactly." He hesitated. "I — I used to hang out with Jess. But it was nothing serious, and it was a long time ago. Now we're just friends." He looked anxiously at me, which made me feel good. He cared what I thought. "Anyway, we were in here and I saw all those yearbooks and I was curious. So I took a look to see if there were any pictures of my mom."

"Do you know where she is now?" I asked.

Ben's eyes clouded over. "She died."

"I'm sorry."

"She died when I was ten."

Poor Ben.

"Are there any pictures?" I said.

He nodded.

"Can I see?"

He hesitated for a moment. Then he ran a hand along a row of yearbooks, pulled one out, thumbed through the pages, and held it out to me.

"That one," he said, pointing at a photograph of a young woman in a formal dress. She was wearing a tiara on her head and was standing arm in arm with a young man wearing a crown. "She was Queen of the Prom," Ben said. His voice was soft and warm.

"She's beautiful," I said. "Actually, you look a lot

like her." He shrugged modestly. "Who's the guy she's with?"

"My dad." His voice had turned cold. He closed the book and slipped it back onto the shelf. "Mr. Duffy was between about sixty and sixty-five. He might even have been a little younger — life on the street ages a person fast. So . . . " He ran his hand backward along the shelf of yearbooks. "What do you say we start here, just to be on the safe side?" He pulled out a stack of yearbooks and carried them to the nearest library table. He pulled out a chair for me and then sat down beside me and watched me leaf through the books. Every time I set one aside, he seemed to slouch a little lower in his chair.

It didn't take long to get through each book. Most of the pictures were of girls — after all, St. Mildred's was a girls' school — so I skipped those. I slowed down only when I got to the pages of photographs that documented the school's co-ed activities — debate competitions, volunteer activities, fundraising events, and school dances. A lot of the pictures on those pages included boys — impossibly clean-cut boys with slicked-back hair and the kind of suits that you see in old movies. I scanned each boy's face but didn't recognize any of them.

I reached for another book.

"Still nothing?" Ben said. "Are you sure you re-member the picture?"

"Pretty sure," I said, paging through yet another volume.

"Talk about a long shot," Ben said. "I mean, it's not

like every girl at St. Mildred's went out with a guy from St. Mark's, and there wouldn't be a photo of every couple anyway. And we don't even know for sure that Mr. Duffy went to St. Mark's. For all we know, he found that ring somewhere . . . "

I heard him talking, but I wasn't really paying attention. I was too busy staring at a photograph — one of half a dozen on the page. It was remarkably similar to the one Ben had just showed me of his mother and father, except that the clothes worn by the young man and young woman looked even more old-fashioned. I tapped the young man's face.

"That's him," I said.

Chapter 14

"Are you sure?" Ben said.

"Positive." The picture hadn't been in my possession for long, but I had studied it and studied it, trying to see Mr. Duffy's face in it. I hadn't succeeded. But the face in that old photograph had branded itself into my brain, and I was certain I was looking at it again now. The young man in this yearbook was the same young man in the small photograph Aisha had given me. In the yearbook picture, he was standing beside an exceptionally pretty young woman. She had arresting eyes that held the camera and made you focus on her to the exclusion of her companion. I looked under the photograph for a caption. There was none. In fact, there were no captions under any of the photographs on the page.

"So close, and yet so far," Ben said.

"If she was at the Prom, then she was a student here," I said. "We can find out her name even if we can't find his."

I flipped back through the yearbook until I came to individual pictures of all the St. Mildred's students that year.

"There she is," I said, pointing triumphantly. "Frances Pfeiffer."

"That's great," Ben said with far less enthusiasm. "But what good does it do? This yearbook is — " He flipped back to the cover. "It's forty-five years old, Robyn."

"Which means that . . . Frances Pfeiffer is sixty-three or sixty-four years old. She's probably still alive, Ben." I stared at the youthful photo and tried to imagine what she might look like now.

"If she is, I'll bet you anything that she got married at some point and changed her name. That's what women did then. How are we going to find her?"

Good question. I thought about it while Ben made photocopies of both pictures — the one of Frances Pfeiffer alone and the one of her with the mystery boy. But it wasn't until we had replaced all the yearbooks and were on our way out of the library that I came up with a plan.

"That woman who gave you the brochure," I said. "Do you know her name?"

"Sure," Ben said. "That was Mrs. Macklin."

"She might be able to help us," I said.

Ben looked doubtful. "Frances Pfeiffer must have graduated at least ten years before Mrs. Macklin," he said. "They've probably never met."

"But when she was talking about raising money for the new computer lab, it sounded like she knew how to get in touch with the school alumnae," I said. "If she doesn't have an address or phone number for Frances Pfeiffer, she might know how to get one."

Ben hunted down a phone book with Pete's help and called Mrs. Macklin. He ended up reaching her voice mail and left a message.

"If she calls me back and if she knows anything, I'll let you know," he told me. He did not sound hopeful.

* * *

My cell phone rang later that night.

"You were right," Ben said. He sounded slightly breathless. "You're so smart, Robyn."

"You mean, Mrs. Macklin thinks she can find out where Frances Pfeiffer is?"

"Better than that. Frances Pfeiffer lives right here in town — she moved back from out west a couple of months ago. Her name is Frances Braithwaite now. Mrs. Macklin gave me her address and phone number. We can contact her tomorrow."

"Let's do it in person," I said. We arranged a time and place to meet.

* * *

The next morning, Ben picked me up and we drove to a very upscale uptown neighbourhood where all the houses were enormous. Ben rang the doorbell and was greeted by a voice that came through a speaker beside the door.

"Yes?" it said.

"We'd like to speak to Mrs. Braithwaite," Ben said.

"Is she expecting you?"

"No," Ben said. "But — "

The front door suddenly opened and a woman, dressed in a coat and boots, stepped out. Her car keys were dangling from one hand.

"I'm Mrs. Braithwaite," she said. She looked to be in her mid-sixties, but her eyes were still as arresting as they had been when she was a student at St. Mildred's, and I could see now that they were a startling pale blue. "But I'm just on my way out, so — "

"My name is Ben Logan," Ben said. "We got your address from Mrs. Macklin at St. Mildred's." Mrs. Braithwaite nodded and smiled politely, but she looked distracted. "My mother went to St. Mildred's," Ben continued. "This is my friend Robyn Hunter."

"I'm sorry," Mrs. Braithwaite said, "but I really have to go."

"This will only take a minute," I said. I pulled one of the photocopied pictures from my bag, smoothed it out, and handed it to her. "Is this you?"

She fished in her handbag for a pair of reading glasses and put them on. Her pale blue eyes widened as she studied the photo.

"Where did you get this?" she said.

"From your high-school yearbook."

"Yes, I can see that. What I mean is, why? What are you doing with this picture?"

"I was hoping you could tell me who the boy is."

She looked at the picture again and her face softened. "His name was Maxwell Templeton."

"*Was?*" Ben said.

"He died a long time ago."

"Are you sure?" I said.

"Quite sure. He's been dead for twenty-two — no, twenty-three — years. Why are you asking — " A cell phone rang. Mrs. Braithwaite pulled one from her coat pocket. "Yes, I know," she said after a moment. "I'm on my way. I'll be there in fifteen minutes." She ended her call. "I really must go," she said. "My daughter is getting married next month and with that and Christmas . . . I'm sorry." She handed the photocopy back to me. For a moment I thought she was going to say something else, but in the end she bustled out to the car that was parked in the driveway, got in, and drove away.

"Well," Ben said as he watched her go, "I think we just hit a dead end."

I looked down at the picture in my hand. Slowly I crumpled it into a ball and jammed it into my coat pocket.

"You did everything you could," Ben said. "In fact, you did more than most people would have. I guess some things just aren't meant to be."

* * *

I had just let myself into my father's loft and had waved to Tara, who was in my father's office, when my cell phone rang. My heart fluttered as I checked the display. Long distance. Was it Nick?

"Hello?" I said breathlessly.

"Hello," came a voice I didn't recognize. The caller identified himself as Doctor Antoski.

"You wanted to talk to me," he said. I didn't know a Dr. Antoski and was about to tell him that he must have the wrong number when he said, "I work at the walk-in clinic on Dennison. I'm in the airport in Nairobi. I just checked my messages and there was one from you. Something about Mr. Duffy."

Now I remembered. Morgan had left a message with my cell phone number for the doctor Mr. Duffy always saw at the walk-in clinic.

"How is Mr. Duffy?" he said.

"I'm afraid he died," I said.

There was a pause on the other end. Then Dr. Antoski said, "How did it happen?"

"He'd been drinking," I said. "They said he passed out."

"If I told him once, I told him a thousand times that it wasn't the street that was going to kill him, it was those litre jugs of cheap red wine that he was always drinking." I heard a heavy sigh on the other end of the line. "I thought I'd finally got through to him. The last time I saw him, he told me he hadn't touched a drop for a couple of months. That was a big deal for someone like him."

I quickly explained why I — well, Morgan — had left a message for him.

"Did Mr. Duffy talk much about himself?" I said.

He seemed to hesitate. "No, not really," he said finally.

"Did he ever talk about his past?"

"Never."

"Not even about what happened to him, about how he'd had that head injury?"

"I asked him a couple of times," Dr. Antoski said. "He'd had one heck of a blow to the head. His skull

190

was caved in on one side. It affected the vision in his left eye, as well as some of his brain function. But he never told me anything about it. I was never sure if that was because he didn't like to talk about it or he didn't remember. It's funny, though. Even with that, he was a whiz with computers. In fact, he helped me with some problems I was having with mine. That's not something you'd expect from a guy his age, let alone a homeless guy his age. Yes, I know grannies are surfing the Net now, but you know what I mean. I'm sorry he's gone. And I'm sorry I can't be more help to you."

Disappointed, I thanked him and disconnected. It looked like Ben was right. Some things weren't meant to be.

Tara came out of my father's office wearing an enormous smile and carrying what looked like a computer case.

"I finally got my computer back," she said. "And it's working! I feel like celebrating." She studied my sombre face. "You look awfully glum. Is everything okay?"

"I've been working on a puzzle," I said. "I was hoping I'd solve it, but . . . " I shrugged.

"How about if I buy us coffee and a decadent dessert?" Tara said. "I know a place that has amazing chocolate-fudge brownies — à la mode, with a hot chocolate sauce to die for. What do you say?"

"Sounds good," I said with as much enthusiasm as I could muster, which wasn't much.

My cell phone rang again. This time it was Aisha.

"I found something else that belonged to Mr. Duffy," she said. "Can you meet me at the coin laundry?"

I said I'd be right there.

"Change of plans?" Tara said.

"I have to meet someone. I'm sorry."

"Is it going to take long?"

"I don't think so."

"Come on, then. I'll drive you to where you're going, and when you're done, we'll get dessert. There's nothing like chocolate when you need a lift."

"Are you sure I'm not messing up your plans?"

"The only plan I had was to celebrate the return of my life-support system," she said. "I can't function without my computer. What do you say, Robyn? You can tell me all about your puzzle. Maybe I can help you work it out."

Tara waited in the car while I went into the laundromat. I found Aisha alone in front of a dryer.

"Rashid is at home watching Yasmin. I told him I had to do the washing early this week — the laundry will be closed on Friday for the holiday." She reached into the pocket of her pathetically thin coat and pulled out a silver locket, which she handed to me. "I found this in Yasmin's drawer," she said. "She says Mr. Duffy gave it to her. The chain is broken. Yasmin says she didn't do it. She says it was broken when Mr. Duffy gave her the locket. He said he wanted her to have it and he made her promise not to tell. He knew that if Rashid found out about it, he would insist that she return it."

I opened the locket. There was a small oval space

inside for a photo. It was empty.

"The picture I gave you," Aisha said. "I think it was originally in this locket. And look." She pointed to the inside cover of the locket, opposite where the picture had been. It had been engraved: *To Franny. Eternally yours, Max.*

"The picture was of a man named Maxwell Templeton," I told Aisha. "And I'm pretty sure that *Franny* must be a woman named Frances Braithwaite. She used to know Maxwell Templeton. She told me he died more than twenty years ago."

"What was Mr. Duffy doing with it?"

"I have no idea."

"Will you return it?" Aisha said.

"Mr. Duffy gave it to Yasmin. Won't she be disappointed?"

Aisha looked squarely at me. "If you know who it belongs to, then please return it," she said. "It's the right thing to do. If someone had given me an engraved locket like that, I would want it back. Wouldn't you?"

* * *

Tara took me to the dessert place she had told me about and ordered lattes and a chocolate-fudge brownie with two spoons. I forced myself to eat some of it, but I think all I accomplished was to dampen Tara's sense of celebration.

"It looks like that puzzle of yours is driving you crazy," she said finally.

"It is," I said. "I hit a dead end and I don't like the feeling."

"I know what you mean," she said. "Why don't you tell me about it? I always feel better when I have a chance to talk things out."

I told her the whole long story.

"I was hoping the picture would turn out to be Mr. Duffy," I said, fingering the locket. "But it looks like another dead end. Or maybe the end of the road. I should have known. The picture didn't look even remotely like him."

"Some people's faces stay perfectly recognizable," Tara said. "But you'd be surprised how much a face can change between sixteen and sixty, especially if a person is ill or had an accident or had a particularly difficult life."

"Maybe," I said. "But the person in my picture turns out to have died over twenty years ago."

"Tough break," Tara said.

We finished our treat and Tara offered to drive me home.

"I have to make another quick stop," I said. I had made a promise to Aisha. Maybe I couldn't find out any more about Mr. Duffy. But I *could* return the locket to its rightful owner — assuming, of course, that she wanted it back. Her name had changed from Pfeiffer to Braithwaite, so she must have gotten married. Maybe she had thrown the locket away years ago. Still . . .

"You go ahead," I said.

"I'll take you," Tara said brightly. "It's the least I can do."

* * *

Mrs. Braithwaite's car was parked in her driveway, which meant that she was home. I hesitated. She was probably busy. She might not be happy to see me — or the locket.

"Problem?" Tara said when I hesitated.

"No." Just do it, I told myself. "I don't think I'll be long."

Tara said that she would wait for me in the car.

This time Mrs. Braithwaite answered the buzzer herself.

When I identified myself and said that I had something of hers, a piece of jewellery, she told me I must be mistaken.

But when I told her it was a locket and read out the inscription, she was silent for a moment, then said, "I'll be right there."

A minute later, the door opened and she admitted me into the foyer. I handed her the locket. She looked at it, opened it, and let out a sort of moan.

"Where did you get this?" she said.

When I told her, she shook her head.

"Is it possible?" she said. "Is it really possible that something you lost more than twenty years ago could suddenly turn up again, thousands of kilometres from where you lost it?"

Lost?

"Mother?" a voice called from the hallway. "I heard the door." A young woman who looked about Tara's age poked her head in. "Oh, I'm sorry," she said, when she saw me. A young man trailed after her. "I heard the door," the young woman said. "I thought it was Edward's father. He should have been here by now."

Mrs. Braithwaite introduced me to her daughter Jenny and to Jenny's fiancé Edward. Jenny looked at her mother again.

"Is everything all right, Mother?" she said.

Mrs. Braithwaite nodded weakly. "Robyn came to return this to me," she said. She handed her daughter the locket.

"The chain is broken," Jenny said.

"I did that," Mrs. Braithwaite said, "just before I threw it at your father."

Jenny looked surprised. "You threw this at Daddy? I don't remember that. I don't remember you two ever arguing, let alone throwing things at each other."

"Look inside, Jenny."

Jenny did as she was told. "Max?" she said. "You mean — "

"I mean your real father, Jenny."

"But he died when I was a baby."

"You were two-and-a-half," Mrs. Braithwaite said, taking the locket back from her daughter. "It should have been the happiest time of our lives and instead it was the unhappiest." She ran her thumb across the surface of the locket. "I didn't think I'd ever see this again," she said to me. "Max and I originally met when we were in school. He was at St. Mark's. I was at St. Mildred's. He was a year older than I was. He gave me this locket in my senior year. It used to have a picture of him inside."

"I know," I said. "I had the picture — and a ring from St. Mark's. That's how I managed to find you."

"You have the picture and his St. Mark's ring?" she asked. "May I see them?"

I explained to her that both the ring and the photograph had been stolen.

Her eyes grew misty as she looked at the locket again. "Max and I planned to get married as soon as we graduated, but my parents thought I was too young. They sent me to Europe for a year. Max went away to university. We wrote to each other for a while and then, I don't know, we just sort of drifted apart. I got married, but it didn't work out. Then one day I ran into Max in an airport, of all places. I hadn't seen him in seventeen years. We had dinner together and it was as if we had never been apart. We got married six months later. Two years after that, just when I thought it would never happen, Jenny came along."

"I don't understand," Jenny said. "If this is your locket, what was *she* doing with it?"

"Someone gave it to me," I said, "and asked me to return it."

"Who?" Mrs. Braithwaite said.

"A woman I know."

"But how did she come to have it? I ripped that locket off my neck and threw it at Max more than twenty years ago. That was the last time I ever saw him or that locket. How did some other woman end up with it?"

"A homeless man gave it to her," I said.

"A homeless man? Where did *he* get it?"

"I don't know."

"Well, does this woman know how to find him? Can we ask him?"

"I'm afraid not," I said. "He died last Monday night. He froze to death."

Mrs. Braithwaite stared at me. "I read about a homeless man who froze to death. Is that the same man?"

I nodded.

"I just don't understand," Mrs. Braithwaite said. "I threw that at Max the last time I saw him. It was never recovered, but I assumed he had it with him when he — " She broke off suddenly, her face twisting in anguish. I felt sorry that I had come. All I had succeeded in doing was stirring up old memories and a lot of pain.

"My father drowned," Jenny said.

"I'm sorry," I said.

"Your father killed himself," Mrs. Braithwaite said quietly.

Jenny stared at her mother. "Killed himself?" she said. "You never told me that."

"It was such a long time ago. You were so young — too young. And Steven was such a good father to you. I didn't think . . . I'm sorry. I should have told you."

Jenny looked at her fiancé, who slipped a protective arm around her.

"I should go," I said quietly, but no one seemed to hear me.

"After you were born," Mrs. Braithwaite said, "I

had a hard time coping. I was home alone all the time. And Max had changed so much in the short time we'd been married. The only thing he ever talked about or seemed to care about was programming and debugging. And he was drinking — far too much for his own good. He was driven by his work — at least, that's what I thought at the time." She glanced at Edward. "Max had such big ideas. He thought he could change the world. He drove himself hard. The last time I saw him, he said he was going to the office. He said he had to think and that he couldn't do that at home with a crying baby and a weepy wife. That's when I yanked the locket off. The chain cut into my neck before it broke. I threw it at him. I was so mad. I told him if work was more important than his own wife and daughter, he could live at the office for all I cared. I was so preoccupied with my own problems that I didn't see what was really going on with him."

"What do you mean?" Jenny said.

"I found out . . . later . . . that he was being treated by a psychiatrist. He'd been drinking so much to deal with his depression. But he kept working. He forced himself. He kept muttering about problems at work, but he never told me what they were, and he never said anything to me about how he was feeling. But I should have seen. I should have noticed." Her eyes filled with tears.

Jenny slipped out of Edward's embrace and hugged her mother.

"His office was in a rundown place near the docks.

He always said he didn't want to waste money on what he called non-essentials. You remember the place, don't you, Edward?"

Edward nodded. "I used to go there with Dad."

"Edward's father and Max were business partners," Mrs. Braithwaite said. Her eyes clouded. "They found Max's watch in the harbour, and his shoes and a few articles of clothing washed up. But they never found his body. They think that maybe the tide . . . The police said there was no evidence of foul play. They knew he'd been in a bar earlier that night. At first they thought maybe he drank too much and fell into the water. When they found out he'd been seeing a psychiatrist, his death was ruled a suicide. I'm sorry, Jenny. I should have told you."

"Mrs. Braithwaite," I said hesitantly. "You said your husband knew about programming and debugging. Was he in the computer business?"

She nodded. "He'd been fascinated by computers ever since he'd heard of them. This was early days in the business, and Max was a real innovator."

"Did you by any chance live out west when you were married to him?"

"Yes," she said. She gave me a curious look. "How did you know?"

I tried to tell myself it was just a coincidence. But I couldn't help thinking about what people had told me — about the daffodils he'd mentioned, the computer magazines he used to read, the photo, the ring, and what Tara had said about hard times changing a person's face.

"I'm pretty sure that Mr. Duffy, the man who froze to death, lived out west for a while. And he knew a lot about computers."

"What are you saying?" said Edward.

"I also know that he was in some kind of accident a long time ago — he'd had a serious head injury. It probably affected his memory."

Mrs. Braithwaite stared at me. "I don't understand," she said.

"You said they never found your husband's body," I said slowly. "So it's possible . . . " My voice trailed off. Was it *really* possible?

"What's possible?" Jenny said.

Mrs. Braithwaite's face turned pale. "You're not suggesting that the man who froze to death was my Max, are you?" She stared at the locket in her hand. "It can't be," she said firmly. Then she looked up at me. "Can it?"

"I don't know," I said. "But there might be a way we can find out."

I told Mrs. Braithwaite, Jenny, and Edward about Tara.

Chapter 15

"Do you have any photographs of Max Templeton before he disappeared, Mrs. Braithwaite?" Tara asked.

Mrs. Braithwaite didn't answer. She still looked pale and rattled.

"I have one," Jenny said. She disappeared from the room and returned a moment later with a framed photograph of a small girl smiling as she sat on the lap of a handsome man who looked like an older version of the boy in the yearbook photo. But he didn't look anything like Mr. Duffy. Maybe I had been wrong. Maybe I was upsetting this woman for nothing. Still . . .

Tara examined it. "Do you have any other pictures?" she asked Mrs. Braithwaite.

Mrs. Braithwaite managed to nod. "But they're still in storage back home. I moved here a few months ago, but not everything has followed me yet."

I pulled the photocopy of the yearbook photo from

my pocket. Tara studied it, frowning a little. "The quality isn't very good," she said. "I don't know if I can use it." Tara looked at Mrs. Braithwaite. "How about photos of any of his relatives? His father or mother. Did he have any siblings?"

"What do you need those for?" Jenny said.

"Well, say the police came to me and wanted me to age the photo of a fugitive who committed a crime, oh, thirty years ago. And say in the photo they give me, the person is twenty-five years old. If I know who the person is, I would try to get photos of some of his closest relatives — brother, sister, father, mother — at age twenty-five, and then at age fifty-five, which is how old the person would be now. That's a big help because it gives me some idea of how the faces of people in his family change as they age and, therefore, how his face might have changed."

Mrs. Braithwaite shook her head. "I don't have anything like that here."

"What about that photo Dad gave you?" Edward said to Jenny. "That might help."

Jenny hurried from the room again and returned with a second photo, this one of two young men flanked by an older couple. I recognized one of the young men as Max Templeton.

"This is my father and Edward's father just after they graduated university," Jenny told Tara. "That's my grandparents with them."

Mrs. Braithwaite looked surprised to see the photograph. "Where did you get that?" she said.

"Edward's father brought it with him. He said he'd

found it while he was cleaning out his office and he thought I'd like to have it."

"It'll be a big help," Tara said. She nodded at a tidy antique desk. "May I set up here?"

Mrs. Braithwaite nodded. Tara unzipped her computer case, pulled out her laptop and a scanner, and set them up on the desk. She scanned the photographs that Jenny had given her.

"Can we watch you work?" I said.

Tara nodded.

We all watched in silence. I was amazed, but not surprised, when the bright-eyed young man in the original photo gradually transformed into an older, more wrinkled and jowlier man. I glanced at Mrs. Braithwaite, who frowned at the image that was taking shape.

"Did Mr. Duffy wear glasses?" Tara asked. "Was he bald? Did he have facial hair — a beard, maybe, or a moustache?"

Mrs. Braithwaite looked at me.

"I don't think he wore glasses," I said. "If he did, I never saw them. He wasn't bald. His hair was long and grey and kind of wavy. Scruffy, too. It hung down over his collar. He didn't have a beard exactly, but the times I saw him, he looked like he needed a shave."

"From what you told me, he was in very poor health," Tara said. "People's health can affect how they age."

"Not only was he homeless, but up until about six months ago, he drank a lot."

"What about that accident he had?" Tara said. "Did it leave any permanent damage — scars, anything like that?"

"His head was caved in on one side," I said. "And he had a scar over and under his left eye." I used a finger to show on my own face what I meant. "His left eye was deformed. It looked like it been twisted."

Tara frowned.

"It was pulled down on one side," I explained. "On the outside."

Tara continued to work. I heard an intake of breath beside me. I turned to Mrs. Braithwaite. Her lips trembled as she watched Tara make adjustments to the image on the screen.

"Like that?" Tara said.

"That scar should be bigger," I said. "And the eye should be kind of scrunched up as well as twisted."

Tara made more adjustments until —

"That's him," I said. "That's Mr. Duffy. That's what he looked like."

"Really?" Tara sounded pleasantly surprised.

"My God," Mrs. Braithwaite said. She swayed on her feet. Jenny and Edward each took one arm and lowered her into a chair. "I've seen that man before," she said. "I dropped money into his hat a few times. But I never spoke to him, and he never said a word to me. And most of the time, he had his head down. Except for once. One time, he looked up at me. I saw all those scars and that ravaged face and I thought, Poor man. I had already dropped some money into his hat and I felt so bad for him that I opened my purse and I gave him a twenty-dollar bill. I don't think I saw him again after that."

"When was that?"

"I don't know," she said. "A few weeks ago, I think."

Edward came over to look at the computer screen. "He looks familiar," he said.

"He always panhandled in front of the same office building downtown," I said. I told him which one.

"That's it," Edward said. "I saw him, too. A couple of times. That's down the street from the company's new offices. That must be where you saw him, too, Frances."

"It was," Mrs. Braithwaite said, her voice weak with shock.

"I remember seeing him a couple of weeks ago. I was going to meet Dad at a restaurant near his office," Edward said. "While I was crossing the street, I saw Dad drop some money into the man's hat. The man said something to Dad." He thought a moment. "Something about a fanny. I remember thinking he must be a bit crazy."

I thought about the name engraved in the locket.

"Are you sure he didn't say Franny?" I said.

"Franny?" He started to shake his head. Then he looked at Mrs. Braithwaite and his eyes widened. "Yes, maybe," he said. "It could have been Franny. I didn't hear clearly."

"Max used to call me Franny," Mrs. Braithwaite said. "He's the only person I've ever let call me that."

"I saw him a second time a few days later. I gave

him money," Edward said. He glanced at Jenny, who was still staring at the computer screen. "I'd better call Dad," Edward said. "He'll want to hear about this." He tried a number, then shook his head. "He's turned his cell phone off. Maybe I can catch him at the hotel." He dug in his pocket, pulled out a business card, and dialled the number on it. "Yes, can you please connect me to room twelve hundred?" While he waited for an answer, the doorbell rang. Jenny went to get it.

"Oh," she said, sounding surprised. "Edward was just calling you."

When she returned a moment later, a man was with her. I was as surprised to see him as he was to see me.

"Mr. Franklin," I said.

"Robyn, isn't it?" he said.

"You two know each other?" Edward said.

"I met Robyn outside the other day," Mr. Franklin said. "She was playing detective." He smiled at me. "I made a donation to your drop-in centre."

"I heard," I said. "They were really happy about that."

"As for the rest of it," he said, "I've asked around the office, but I'm afraid I wasn't able to discover anything. A few people remembered the man, but nobody had spoken to him." He glanced at Tara and then turned to his son, clearly waiting for an introduction, which Edward quickly supplied.

"Dad, *we've* just discovered something," Edward said. "At least, I think we have."

"That homeless man who froze to death," Mrs. Braithwaite said, her voice trembling. "James . . . we think it might have been Max."

"*Max?*" Mr. Franklin stared at her as if she had just announced that she was really the Queen of England. "What do you mean?"

Jenny filled him in.

"That's preposterous," Mr. Franklin said when she had finished.

He looked at Mrs. Braithwaite. His tone was softer when he spoke to her. "Frances, it can't be Max. Max is dead. This picture — " He nodded at the computer screen. "It's not even science."

"It's not conclusive," Tara said. "But it is pretty accurate. There are more reliable steps you can take to confirm his identity. DNA, for example."

"But his body was never found," Mrs. Braithwaite said to Mr. Franklin. "What if he didn't commit suicide? What if something happened to him? Robyn said he had a serious head injury. What if he didn't die but had some kind of terrible accident? What if he didn't come home because he *couldn't?* My God, what if his funeral was only last week?" Tears streamed down her cheeks.

Jenny hugged her mother tightly. "You couldn't have known."

"You can't seriously think Max has been alive all this time," Mr. Franklin said.

"Look, Dad," Edward said, turning Tara's computer around so that his father could take a good look at the face on the screen. "We saw this man, remember? He said something to you about Franny. Remember?"

"We *saw* this man?"

"You gave him money."

"Did I?" Mr. Franklin shook his head. "I don't remember." He studied the image on Tara's computer screen. "That cannot possibly be Max," he insisted.

"There's a very good chance it is," Tara said.

"He froze to death, James," Mrs. Braithwaite said. "Max froze to death. On the street. Only a few kilometres from where we are right now."

"First things first, Frances. We don't even know for sure that this man was Max. But I'm sure there are ways to find out, like this young woman said. There must be steps we can take. But, Frances, really, it seems highly unlikely that that man was Max."

"But what if he was?"

"If he was, we'll deal with it. But Jenny is right — you couldn't have known. For heaven's sake, I apparently dropped money into his hat and I didn't recognize him, either. Certainly no one can fault *you*, Frances. You're one of the most generous people I know. Look at how many charities you support, how many committees you sit on. If it will make you feel better, you can make a donation to that drop-in centre of Robyn's. You can help to make sure that no one else has to freeze to death in this city." He looked at me. "How can such a thing happen? How can a man freeze to death in the middle of a big city like this? It just doesn't seem right."

"According to the pathologist, Mr. Duffy had had a lot to drink that evening. He passed out. He only had one thin blanket over him. That's why he froze to death."

"Drinking?" Mr. Franklin shook his head again. "Well, that sounds like Max. He never could resist his Napoleon, could he, Frances?"

That wasn't entirely true, I thought. According to Aggie and Dr. Antoski, he hadn't had a drink in months. Why had he chosen the coldest night of the year to slide back into his old behaviour? I hoped it wasn't because he had been barred from the drop-in centre.

Mrs. Braithwaite wiped her tears and turned to Tara. "Who can we contact?" she said. "Who can help us prove this one way or the other?"

Chapter 16

"I wasn't kidding," my father said. "You're a natural." He looked up from the newspaper and beamed proudly at me. "And, if you ask me, they should have put your picture in the paper along with those pictures of Max Templeton."

The story hadn't made the front page, but it was Christmas Eve and a slow news day, so the paper had run a longish article that described the photographic ageing that Tara had done and then detailed some of Maxwell Templeton's known history. It showed four photos of him — the two Jenny had provided, the one Tara had created, and the group photo from the drop-in centre, enlarged to show a grainy image of Mr. Duffy's face after years of living on the street. The article mentioned that James Franklin was Max Templeton's former business partner and now a major shareholder, along with Mrs. Braithwaite, of the company he and Max Templeton had founded.

"Mrs. Braithwaite phoned me," I said. "She had

some of Max's things taken from storage. Apparently somewhere in there was a box he'd got from his mother — his first pair of shoes, a silver baby cup, *and* the first tooth he ever lost. She found a private lab that will do a DNA analysis for her — although she seems pretty sure now that Mr. Duffy and Max were the same person."

My father kept right on beaming. "And she owes it all to my little girl," he said.

"I'm glad I could help," I said. "But it's such a sad story. Poor Mr. Duffy. He had such a hard life. He lost so much. And to think that he and Mrs. Braithwaite actually saw each other, and she didn't even recognize him." I shook my head. I felt so sorry for both of them.

"Head injuries can be pretty dicey," my father said. "People's personalities can change dramatically and their memory can be seriously impaired."

"You know what bothers her the most — besides the fact that she was face to face with him after twenty-three years and didn't even know it? The fact that she'll probably never know what happened to him — how he got hurt and why he never contacted her."

My father shook his head. "Some mysteries are a lot harder to solve than others."

"She also says that Mr. Franklin feels terrible that he didn't recognize Mr. Duffy either. He thought Mr. Duffy was just ranting — he never made the link between Mr. Duffy mentioning the name Franny and Mrs. Braithwaite."

"Well, *you* did a good job, Robbie."

"I guess," I said. "But I feel like I only found out half of Mr. Duffy's story."

"You know what they say — half a loaf is better than none."

True, I guess. I glanced at my watch. "I gotta go, Dad, or I'm going to be late. Ben's waiting for me."

My father gave me a mischievous grin. "Ben again, huh?"

I shrugged, but I couldn't keep myself from smiling just a little. When I had told Ben what had happened — that Mrs. Braithwaite was almost positive that Mr. Duffy was Max Templeton and that she was going to get a DNA test to prove it — he had grabbed me and hugged me tightly. When he'd finally let me go, he'd looked into my eyes and said, "Boy, was I ever wrong about you." And then, just like that, he'd kissed me. And I'd kissed him back. Just like that. Without even thinking about it. Later, when I was in bed, I thought about Nick — about how it had felt when I was with him and how sure I had been that he loved me. But he was gone. He'd been gone for weeks. He hadn't called even once. Maybe that's why when I closed my eyes that night, I was thinking of Ben, not Nick.

"We're going to the drop-in centre," I told my father now. "Some kids are coming in to decorate a Christmas tree." And tomorrow, before Mom and Ted and I had Christmas dinner, Ben, Billy, Morgan, and I were going to serve turkey dinners at the drop-in centre.

"Will you be back for supper?"

I nodded.

"Do me a favour? Pick up some olive oil, will you? I'm all out."

I said that I would.

* * *

A lot of heads turned when Ben and I arrived at the drop-in centre. Mr. Donovan spotted us from across the hall and strode toward us, smiling. He shook my hand and congratulated me on what I had done. So did Betty. Andrew was holding a copy of the newspaper and seemed to be studying it. He came up to me and quietly said, "That was good what you did."

"Thank you, Andrew."

Betty asked me how I had managed to get so much information on a man as quiet as Mr. Duffy, so I explained how Morgan and I had trudged all around the neighbourhood and spoken to anyone who might have known him, how I'd made a sign and stood where Mr. Duffy panhandled to gather information from passersby, how Ben and I had tracked down Mrs. Braithwaite . . .

"It's so weird about Mrs. Braithwaite, though," Ben said, not for the first time. "She actually gave him money but didn't recognize him."

"So did James Franklin," I said.

"And that guy," Andrew said, nodding at the newspaper.

"What guy?" I said.

Andrew tapped James Franklin's face. *"That* guy."

"That's James Franklin," I said. "See?" I pointed to his name, which was printed in the caption under the photo. Was it my imagination or did Andrew look

214

embarrassed? "He and Max went to school together and then were in business together. Max even spoke to James Franklin and Mr. Franklin didn't recognize him."

"Max?" Andrew said. "Who's Max?"

"Max Templeton. That was Mr. Duffy's real name," I said. The headline above the photos read: *Homeless man revealed as computer whiz Max Templeton.* I was beginning to get a clue as to at least one reason Andrew was on the street.

"He gave him something else, too," Andrew said. "And Mr. Duffy shoved him away. Remember?"

"Who gave who something? What are you talking about, Andrew?" Ben said.

"Remember, Robyn?" Andrew said. "I told you I saw a man trying to give Mr. Duffy something, and Mr. Duffy yelled at him?" I did remember. He had told me the day Morgan and I had come down to the drop-in centre to start asking about Mr. Duffy. "That was the guy," Andrew said. He pointed again at James Franklin's face.

That didn't sound right. Edward had seen his father give money to Mr. Duffy, and he'd said that Mr. Duffy had mentioned the name Franny. But he hadn't said anything about Mr. Duffy yelling at him. Nor had Mr. Franklin.

"Are you sure that's the same man, Andrew?" I said.

He nodded.

"Did you see another man with him? A younger man?"

Andrew shook his head.

"I don't get it," Ben said. "Are you saying that Mr. Franklin gave Mr. Duffy money, and Mr. Duffy yelled at him?"

I thought back to what Andrew had told Morgan and me.

"Mr. Duffy collected money in a hat, didn't he?" I said.

Andrew nodded.

"And people dropped money into the hat, right?"

Another nod.

"But you said the man you saw — Mr. Franklin — was trying to give Mr. Duffy something. What did you mean, Andrew?"

"He was trying to put something in his hand."

"In his hand — not in his hat?"

"In his hand," Andrew said.

"You're sure?"

"I know what I saw."

"And you said that you saw that happen a couple of days before Mr. Duffy died, right, Andrew?" I said. I was pretty sure that's what he had said.

"It was the day before you came to the drop-in centre for the first time," Andrew said.

"What's going on, Robyn?" Ben asked. "Is something wrong?"

"I don't know. Probably not," I said. But something was bothering me. Edward had said that he had encountered Mr. Duffy twice. But James Franklin remembered seeing Mr. Duffy only once, and he'd remembered only *after* Edward had reminded him.

He hadn't volunteered that he'd seen him again. It's possible that it had slipped his mind. But after that first time he would surely have remembered a face like Mr. Duffy's, wouldn't he, especially if he'd been trying to give him something and Mr. Duffy had been resisting? "You didn't see what he was giving him, did you, Andrew? Was it money?"

Andrew thought hard. "I don't know. But I guess it was money. That's what most people give us — if they give us anything at all. Sometimes someone will give us food or a cup of coffee, but that guy wasn't doing that."

"Why would Mr. Duffy refuse to take money?" Ben said.

It was a good question, one that nagged at me for the rest of the day and that was still on my mind when Ben drove me back to my father's place. He came upstairs and I introduced him to my father, who promptly invited him to stay for supper — "Unless you're expected home," he added, "this being Christmas Eve."

Ben glanced at me.

"I can stay," he said. "Thank you."

We all went into the kitchen where my father had already started grilling chicken for his famous Cajun chicken wraps. Ben offered to help. My father handed us each a knife and gestured toward the heap of salad vegetables on the counter. While we washed and sliced cucumber, celery, green onions, peppers, and tomatoes, Ben and my father chatted about sports and school. They seemed to be getting along great —

just like Nick and my father had. A wave of sadness and anger washed over me. But Ben was here, and Nick wasn't. And that wasn't my fault.

"Now for the salad dressing," my father said. He looked expectantly at me.

"What?" I said.

"I asked you to bring home some olive oil. Tell me you remembered, Robbie."

"Oh, no!" I gave him a distressed look. My father looked exasperated — for a split second.

"Nice try," he said. "Where is it?"

"In my bag." I went to fetch it. The two paperback novels that Mr. Duffy had bought from the library were sitting on a small table beside the door, where I had left them. I didn't even know why I had hung onto them. I looked at them now, and at the small rectangle of stiff paper that was sticking out of one of them — the business card that Mr. Duffy had been using as a bookmark. The business card of one of the best hotels in town. I pulled it from between the pages and stared at it.

"Robbie, do you think I could have that olive oil sometime before the start of the new year?" my father called from the kitchen.

I walked slowly back to the kitchen with the card in my hand.

"Robbie?" my father said. "Are you okay?"

"This is the hotel where James Franklin is staying," I said. "His son phoned him while I was at Mrs. Braithwaite's. He had the same business card."

My father gave me a peculiar look.

"We found this card in one of Mr. Duffy's books," I said. "Remember, Ben?"

Ben nodded.

"Mr. Franklin is staying at this hotel. Edward says he saw his father give money to Mr. Duffy and heard Mr. Duffy say the name Franny a couple of *weeks* ago. Andrew — he's the guy I told you about from the drop-in centre, Dad — he saw Mr. Franklin give something to Mr. Duffy a couple of days *before* he died. Don't you see? Andrew saw Mr. Franklin and Mr. Duffy together. He saw Mr. Franklin trying to give Mr. Duffy something *after* Mr. Franklin had already seen Mr. Duffy once and *after* Mr. Duffy had mentioned the name Franny, but just *before* Mr. Duffy died. I don't think it was money, because if it was, he would have dropped it into Mr. Duffy's hat. But he didn't do that. Andrew said he saw Mr. Franklin try to put something into Mr. Duffy's hand."

"What are you saying, Robbie?"

"I'm not sure." But I was thinking fast. "What was Mr. Duffy doing with a card to the hotel where Mr. Franklin was staying? How did he get it unless Mr. Franklin *gave* it to him?"

"You think that's what Andrew saw — Mr. Franklin giving a business card to Mr. Duffy?" Ben said.

I nodded. "But why would Mr. Franklin give the business card of the hotel where he was staying to a homeless man he claimed he didn't know and didn't even really look at?"

Ben looked baffled. My father looked thoughtful.

"What exactly do you know about James Franklin?" he said.

"Not much," I admitted. "He seemed nice the first time we met him, didn't he, Ben?"

"The first time?" my father said. "You mean, at Mrs. Braithwaite's house?"

"No. I met him before that. We both did, two days before the funeral, when we were trying to find people who might have given Mr. Duffy money and who might have spoken to him." I described how Mr. Franklin had approached me in front of the office building, and how I'd told him all about the drop-in centre and how Ben and I volunteered there. "He made a donation," I said. "A big one."

"So he knew who you were and that you volunteered at the drop-in centre," my father said. "And that you were trying to find out who Mr. Duffy was." He thought about that for a few moments. "After you first met James Franklin, did you notice anything unusual?"

"Like what?"

"Like maybe someone taking a special interest in you?"

I shook my head.

"What about the night you were mugged?"

That's when it hit me.

"There was this guy who showed up at the funeral," I said. "That was the day after Ben and I met Mr. Franklin for the first time. This man sat near me at the funeral. I'd never seen him before." I described everything that I remembered about the man in the black tuque. "He was also at the drop-in centre the night I got mugged, when Andrew was showing the ring and the picture around. At first I thought he was a client. But then I realized that he couldn't be because I saw him get into a car and drive away as I was leaving. What if . . . " I felt the hair stand up on the back of my neck. Then I shook my head. "He left before me. So he couldn't have followed me."

"That's not necessarily true," my father said. "James Franklin found out who you were and what you were doing two days before the funeral. Suppose he hired someone to check you out, maybe follow you."

I was beginning to get a sick feeling in the pit of my stomach.

"If he did, that person would know that you travelled by bus. The best way I know to make someone think they're not being followed is to get out in front of them. He left before you, but I bet he was watching you at the bus stop and I bet when you got into that taxi, he followed you."

"You think he's the one who mugged Robyn?" Ben said, incredulous.

"Whoever took your purse kept the money and the ring, which makes sense. They're worth something," my father said. "They tossed everything else. We found your wallet, your ID, and a few other items. But we never found that picture. You want to tell me why a purse-snatcher would keep a useless old photograph?"

I looked at my father. I knew he was thinking the same thing I was.

"Someone wanted to stop me from finding out who Mr. Duffy really was," I said.

"Could be," my father said.

My mind was racing now.

"Do you remember that bottle I saw, Dad?"

My father nodded slowly.

"What bottle?" Ben said.

I told him about the empty cognac bottle that had rolled out of the alley right beside where Billy and I had found Mr. Duffy.

"It was the same brand my dad likes," I said.

"Napoleon," my father said, smiling fondly. "Fine stuff."

"You remember what you said, Dad? You said you'd be surprised if a homeless person could afford to buy that brand."

"Well, it's top-of-the-line stuff, Robbie. Why? What are you thinking?"

"I told Mr. Franklin that Max froze to death after passing out from too much alcohol, and do you know what he said?" Both Ben and my father were looking intently at me now. "He said, 'Max never could resist his Napoleon.'"

"Well, he *did* know the man," my father said. "They started a business together. They worked together." But I could tell he was thinking it all through.

"People told Morgan and me that Mr. Duffy had quit drinking. And the doctor he used to see at the walk-in clinic said that when Mr. Duffy drank, it was cheap red wine. And you said the cognac he drank the night he died was expensive."

"Extremely expensive," my father said.

We looked at each other.

"There's one more thing, Dad," I said. "Mr. Duffy used to warm up at a place called the Black Cat Café. One of the guys who worked there let Mr. Duffy use the phone sometimes. He said Mr. Duffy made a call from there a couple of days before he died."

"Does he know who Mr. Duffy called?"

I shook my head.

"What's going on?" Ben said.

"Watch the chicken, Robbie," my father said, reaching for the phone. He talked to an old friend of his on the homicide squad. An hour later, Will Spivak, came over to ask my father and me some questions.

* * *

I spent Christmas Day with my mother, as usual, and had brunch with my father at La Folie the next day — our own post-split-up tradition.

The Tuesday after Christmas, my father showed up at my mother's house. She was not pleased by the surprise visit, mostly because my mother had taken a few days off work and Ted was there with us.

"Relax, Patti," my father said. "I'm not staying long. I just want to talk to Robbie." He spotted me over her shoulder.

"Do you want to tell me why you didn't call me when Robyn was mugged?" my mother said. She had not been pleased when I had told her.

My father glanced at me. "Robbie wanted to tell you herself," he said. "She handled herself well."

"She was mugged," my mother said.

"I'm fine, Mom," I said — again. I'd said it a million times already.

"I just need a minute with Robbie," my father said. He looked at me. "Will called me."

"Mom, let him come in. Please."

"Who's Will?" my mother said.

"Spivak. You remember him, Patti."

I guess she did because she stepped aside to let my father in out of the cold.

"You were right, Robbie," he said. "James Franklin received a phone call in his hotel room shortly after six the night Max Templeton died. Within minutes he was downstairs getting the doorman to hail him a taxi. Will tracked down the driver and showed him some photos. The driver remembered James Franklin. He says he drove him to a liquor store and then dropped him off in front of a place called the Black Cat Café."

"Mr. Duffy used to go there sometimes," I explained to my mother and Ted.

"That's exactly what the counterman told Will," my father said. "And it turns out Mr. Duffy used the phone that night. He called James Franklin's hotel — shortly after six."

"Did the counterman see Mr. Franklin?"

My father shook his head. "But he says Mr. Duffy was watching at the window, and he remembers seeing a cab. But it was a busy night — a lot of people were in the place trying to stay warm. He didn't pay any attention to it. Mr. Duffy left right after that."

"What's this all about?" my mother said, curious despite herself.

"Sounds like a murder mystery to me," Ted said jovially.

"Max Templeton and James Franklin were business partners. Max's wife said Max was having some kind of problem at work. Then Max goes out one night, never comes back, and is presumed dead — a suicide. But he didn't die. Instead, it turns out he had a serious accident that left him with a brain injury and facial disfigurement, and he was never seen or heard from again — until more than twenty years later," my father said. "I wonder what kind of problems he was having at work."

"You think maybe that first accident wasn't an accident?" I said.

"You mean I was right?" Ted said, his smile replaced by a look of astonishment. "We're actually talking about a murder?"

"Could be," my father said. "Say, is that eggnog?" He headed for the dining room table where my mother had been laying out brunch.

My mother opened her mouth to protest. She closed it again when Ted said, "It sure is. I was just going to pour myself one. Join me, Mac?" My mother sighed heavily.

Chapter 17

Ben and I spent the last day of the year at the drop-in centre, doing food preparation and playing cards with some of the regulars. I kept an eye out for Andrew. When I saw him come in, I excused myself from the card game and went over to him.

"Hey, Robyn," he said. He started to smile and then stopped himself, as usual.

"Go ahead," I said. "Do it."

"Do what?"

"Give me a great big smile."

He shook his head.

"Come on, Andrew," I said. "Let yourself go."

He shook his head. "I can't."

"Why not?"

He looked down at the ground.

"It's your teeth, isn't it, Andrew?"

He nodded without raising his head.

"Come on, smile for me. Please?"

His head came up slowly and, after a moment's hesitation, he allowed himself to smile, but there was no genuine emotion behind it. As he showed me his teeth, his cheeks turned red and he looked down again.

"Teeth can be fixed, Andrew," I said.

"Getting them fixed costs money."

"Dentistry students are always looking for people to practise on. They don't charge much. Some of them do some free work, too, for people who can't afford it. I checked it out for you and I found someone who will help you out. I can make you an appointment, if you'd like."

This time when he looked at me, he did smile, widely and spontaneously. He started to raise his hand to cover his mouth, but I caught it and held it down.

"Thanks, Robyn," he said.

"Happy New Year, Andrew," I said. Maybe after his teeth were fixed and he had a little more confidence, we could work on his reading problem.

At five o'clock, Ben and I headed over to my father's place to help set up for his annual New Year's Eve party. Morgan and Billy were planning to come, as were some of my father's tenants, his business associates, and practically everyone he knew.

The buzzer sounded while my father and Ben were hanging streamers and a *Happy New Year* banner.

"Get that, will you, Robbie?" my father said.

It was Mrs. Braithwaite.

"I'm sorry," she said when she saw the party preparations. "I don't want to interrupt. I just wanted to tell you in person — "

My father scrambled down from the stepladder he had been standing on and came over to introduce himself.

"We spoke on the phone," he said. He turned to me. "Will gave Mrs. Braithwaite my number. She asked if she could drop by to see you." He waved her inside. "Can I offer you something to drink, Mrs. Braithwaite?"

"Please, call me Frances," she said. "Mr. Hunter — "

"Mac," my father said.

Mrs. Braithwaite smiled, but there was sadness in her eyes. "Mac. I just wanted to thank you and your daughter for everything. James . . . " She hesitated and drew in a deep breath. "The police have arrested James for Max's murder."

So I had been right — Mr. Duffy's death hadn't been an accident. I glanced at my father, but couldn't tell what he was thinking.

"The prosecutor offered to reduce the charge from first-degree to second-degree and to recommend eligibility for parole after ten years if he confessed," Mrs. Braithwaite said.

"Ten years?" I said. It didn't seem like much after what he had done. "Did he take it?"

Mrs. Braithwaite nodded. "James is sixty-three years old. If he were convicted of first-degree murder, he'd have spent the rest of his life in prison. At least this way he has a chance of getting out before he dies."

My father nodded, but didn't say anything. Mrs. Braithwaite continued.

"James told the police that he thought he'd killed Max twenty-three years ago," she said.

"But why?" Ben asked. "What did he have against Mr. Duffy — I mean, Mr. Templeton?"

"Max and James were in business together. The computer business. They did very well. They both made a lot of money. Then Max developed a new program that would have made them more money — a *lot* more. But Max wasn't interested in making more money. I remember him telling me that if money was all he was interested in, he could have retired years ago. He wanted to make sure that anyone who wanted to use his new program could have it."

"And Mr. Franklin didn't like that," I said.

"No, he didn't," Mrs. Braithwaite said. "He says he tried to reason with Max. But Max was having problems by then. He was seeing a psychiatrist, and he was drinking. He threatened to break up the partnership and take his new program with him."

"Is that why Mr. Franklin killed him?" Ben said.

"He couldn't bear the thought of Max giving away something that was so valuable. The last night I saw Max, we had a big fight. Max said he was going to the office. He had set up the business down near the docks where the rents were cheap. The area was surrounded by warehouses. James was waiting for him. He clubbed Max with a piece of pipe, then removed all of his identification and some of his clothing."

"He obviously overlooked a few items," my father said. "The locket and the ring."

"He said he heard someone coming, and he panicked. He had to hurry. He dumped Max's body in a truck behind one of the warehouses. The truck was taking a shipment south, across the border. He hid Max at the very back of the truck, under some old packing blankets where he would have less chance of being spotted — assuming anyone even searched the truck. Security was a lot more lax back then. Then he threw some of Max's things into the water."

"To support the theory of suicide," my father said.

"Where did Mr. Duf— Mr. Templeton end up?" Ben said.

"No one knows," Mrs. Braithwaite said. "I'm going to hire someone to see if I can find out. All I know at this point is that Max suffered massive head trauma. He may have had brain damage and some loss of his memory." She shook her head. "If only I had known. If only he had found some way to contact me."

"It must have been a shock to Mr. Franklin to run into Max after all these years," I said.

"It was," Mrs. Braithwaite said. "He thought Max had been dead for years. He says he didn't even recognize him. It was Max who spoke first. He told James that he'd seen me — well, that he'd seen Franny. Even then James didn't recognize him. To him, Max was just some filthy homeless man muttering about Franny. Then James saw the locket. He tried to take it from Max."

"No wonder Max gave it to Aisha," I said. "He told her that he was afraid it would be stolen."

"James said he was thunderstruck. He says he

looked at him again and started to see how it could be Max. They went all through school together, did you know that? Max even had his old school ring. And then Edward came along, and James hustled him away before Max could say anything else."

"But Edward heard him say your name," I said.

"Which meant nothing to Edward. He's always known me as Frances. And he would never have recognized Max." Mrs. Braithwaite's voice trembled.

"Let me get you some water, Frances," my father said gently.

Mrs. Braithwaite shook her head. "No, but thank you."

"Why didn't Mr. Franklin just avoid Mr. Templeton?" Ben said. "Why did he kill him?"

"Fear," Mrs. Braithwaite said. "Max had mentioned my name. He had the locket. He'd said he'd seen me. He said something about wanting to go home."

"He said something like that to Aisha," I said. "He asked her if she would take him back. She didn't know what he was talking about. But maybe he was talking about *you*. Maybe he was wondering if you'd take him back after all these years and after everything that had happened to him."

Mrs. Braithwaite's eyes were misty as she nodded. "James was also afraid that someone would find out who Max really was and what James himself had done all those years ago. He kept an eye on Max for the next little while."

"And then he killed him," Ben said.

Mrs. Braithwaite nodded. "James tried to get

friendly with Max so that he could try to find out what Max remembered."

"He gave Max a card from the hotel where he was staying," I said. "Did he say why he did that?"

"For the same reason," Mrs. Braithwaite said. "If Max contacted him, that would mean he really did remember something, that he really did want to go home. When Max didn't contact him, James started to think that everything was going to be okay."

"But he did call," I said. "He called the night he died."

Mrs. Braithwaite's eyes teared up again. "He was cold. He wanted a place to stay."

No wonder. It had been the coldest night of the year.

"So he called James. And that's when James saw his chance. He arranged to meet Max. On the way, he picked up a bottle of Max's favourite drink."

"Cognac," I said. "Napoleon."

Mrs. Braithwaite nodded again. "He told Max it was just a short walk to the hotel. He said he'd brought something to keep them warm on the way. He kept Max drinking until he passed out. It couldn't have taken long, with Max in the shape he was. Then James left him in a doorway and watched him for a while from across the street to make sure he didn't move." She wiped tears from her eyes. "He was also responsible for what happened to you, Robyn. When he heard what you were doing, he had you followed."

By the man in the black tuque.

"When he found out you had that photo, he was

afraid it might come to light and that someone — me, I suppose — might recognize it. He paid someone to take it away from you. I'm sorry. But he's given the police the man's name. If they can find him, they'll arrest him for robbery and assault."

I didn't know what to say.

"Well, at least I know what happened to poor Max," Mrs. Braithwaite said. "And I know because someone — you, Robyn — cared enough about one of society's rejects to try to put a human face on him. I'll always be grateful for that."

"It was Ben's idea," I said.

"But Robyn did all the work," Ben said. He slipped an arm around me. My father raised an eyebrow.

"You both deserve a lot of credit," my father said. "Are you sure I can't tempt you with some eggnog, Frances?"

"Jenny and Edward are waiting for me," she said. "Poor Edward — he's shattered by what his father did. But Jenny is standing by him. And Edward is going to carry on with the business."

* * *

After Mrs. Braithwaite left, we finished the party preparations. It wasn't long before my father's guests started to arrive. My father, being my father, put on some old rock and roll — and a lot of Motown — and managed to get almost everyone up and dancing.

When it was nearly midnight, Ben looked around. The music was quieter now as everyone started to anticipate the countdown to the New Year. Morgan and Billy were swaying to the song that was playing and were gazing dreamily into each other's eyes. I spotted Vern and his girlfriend Henri (short for Henrietta) with their arms around each other.

"It's a fun party," Ben said. He looked around, checking, I think, to see where my father was — on the far side of the living room with a couple of his cop friends. Then he pulled me into the kitchen where we were shielded from view, wrapped his arms around me, pulled me closer, and kissed me. The party sounds disappeared. All I heard was my heart beating in my chest. All I felt was the warmth of Ben's arms around me. Then I heard my father's booming voice.

"Look who's finally here!" he was saying. "Tara! Come in. Come in."

A few moments later Tara appeared in the kitchen. Ben and I jumped apart as if we'd both been jolted with a cattle prod. Tara giggled.

"Sorry," she said. "If there'd been a door, I would have knocked. I was just looking for something to toast the New Year with."

When I introduced her to Ben, she gave me a furtive thumbs up.

"Oh, hey, did you get that package, Robyn?" she said.

"Package?"

"A package came addressed to you. I had to sign for it. I left it — " She paused to think. "I left it on top of the fridge," she said, spinning around. "And there it is." She reached for it and handed it to me.

It was a small box wrapped in brown paper. My

name and my father's address were printed neatly on it, but there was no return address.

"Open it," Ben said.

I tore off the paper and lifted the lid off the box. Nestled inside was a gold pendant in the shape of two intertwined hearts.

"Hey," Ben said. "Don't tell me you have a secret admirer!"

I laughed. "As if you didn't know what it was!"

"I didn't," Ben said. "It's not from me."

I laughed again.

"Really, Robyn," he said. "It's not from me."

I got a strange feeling.

I turned the pendant over. The engraving on the back read: *To RH. Love you forever. ND.*

Nick.

"So?" Ben said, smiling. "Who's it from? Do I have a reason to be jealous?"

I put the pendant back into the box and closed the lid. "No," I said. "You don't."

Other great books
by Norah McClintock

Robyn Hunter Mysteries
Last Chance
You Can Run
Nothing to Lose
Out of the Cold
Shadow of Doubt

Chloe and Levesque Mysteries
The Third Degree
Over the Edge
Double Cross
Scared to Death
Break and Enter
No Escape
Not a Trace

Mike and Riel Mysteries
Hit and Run
Truth and Lies
Dead and Gone
Seeing and Believing
Dead Silence

Also available
Body, Crime, Suspect
The Body in the Basement
Password: Murder
Mistaken Identity